# *ISAIAH'S TEARS*

# ISAIAH'S TEARS

## Book Two of the Savannah Stories

*by*

# ROBERT T.S. MICKLES, Sr.
## *with a foreword by Aberjhani*

ALSO BY ROBERT T.S. MICKLES, SR.


*Blood Kin, A Savannah Story (2007)*

# Isaiah's Tears

First Edition

Lulu Special Run ISBN 9781435743663

Manufactured in the United States of America

*To my father, Jordan Thomas Tremble, who as I grew up allowed me to be me, and whom I will always love and respect.*

# ♦ FOREWORD ♦

In his *ESSENCE* Magazine bestseller, *Blood Kin, A Savannah Story*, Robert T.S. Mickles introduced readers all over the world to the residents of Woodloe Plantation as they grappled with the violent chaos of the Civil War and struggled to adapt to the changes taking place in their lives as well as to simply survive. For best friends Lew and Robert, one of the greatest changes they experienced was the fantastic discovery that they were brothers, both of them sons of Master Jones, one of them free, one of them a slave.

  While no one could ever be so naïve as to deny the dehumanizing horrors of slavery as it was often practiced in the United States during the 1700s and 1800s, Mickles was bold enough to share with us a story that his grandmother, Mrs. Beulah Tremble, a daughter of slaves, had shared with him. It allowed for a different perspective on America's "peculiar institution" and has stimulated within classrooms fresh dialogues on the full meaning and impact of that same institution.

In *Isaiah's Tears*, part two of the author's *Savannah Stories*, we meet fifteen-year-old Isaiah Jones. For Isaiah, the end of slavery in the United States in 1865 means the beginning of a long but very challenging life as a free man. In the pages that follow, Isaiah shares the story of that life with a group of friends from Howard University in Washington, D.C. And what a story it is!

Following the death of both his parents and the acquisition of his sudden unexpected freedom, Isaiah has to choose between life as he has always known it—and life as an uncertain adventure in a new and uncertain world. He makes a solemn pledge to keep his remaining family safe and help them establish new lives as free individuals.

His story is at times laugh-out-loud comical and at other times heartbreakingly tragic. As a reader, one cannot help but whisper little encouragements and at times hold one's breath while watching Isaiah grow from an adolescent who had never expected to be anything but a slave in his life to a young man anticipating a future with his new wife, an infant daughter, and his aunt and her children. He recounts his determination to work the fields of Woodloe Plantation until saving up enough money to move his family North, then settling in Washington, D.C. However, neither freedom nor money, he discovers, can guarantee safety or happiness.

As evidenced by the quotes on the back of this book, Mickles' debut novel, *Blood Kin, A Savannah Story*, won him the kind of acclaim that most first-time authors only hope to receive and that even many veteran authors have rarely experienced. As he did in that first installment of his *Savannah Stories*, Mickles delivers in *Isaiah's Tears* an amazing tale that says as much about who Americans have been in the past as it does about who we are right now, a people intent on making the concepts of freedom, democracy, and "the pursuit of happiness" as real in practice as they are meaningful in concept.

Author-Poet Aberjhani
author of *The American Poet Who Went Home Again*
July 2008

# ♦ PROLOGUE ♦

I was born right here on Woodloe Plantation, and so were my daddy, and his daddy before him, and his daddy before him. People tells us we from Africa, but this plantation the only thing I know about being anywhere from. I ain't never set one foot off it. Don't rightly know if I ever wants to. Some of us like that storyteller Old Jordan, and Master's slave son Robert, have gone off it. They told us how it was in Savannah just down the road.

Then again there was that time when the Confederate soldiers took some men from here to work down by the Savannah River. That was when I lost my daddy. He never came back to the plantation after that. Master Jones' white son Lew had to go and get the rest of them. Five of them never come back home. My daddy was one of the five. I never got over the fact that it was Mrs. Jones' son Isaac, who wasn't one of my Master Jones' sons like Lew and Robert, it was his bragging that got my daddy taken from me. I miss him still today. Even though it's been a couple'a years now since he passed, it feels like it was only yesterday.

No I don't think I ever wants to leave here, this is

my home. But now they telling us we all free and can go. Go where? Down that road to Savannah where my daddy died so I can die there too? I've heard tell more than once how white peoples treats us and kills us. Here at Woodloe, Master Jones and Lew always been pretty regular with us. I never knowed nothing to complain about 'til Isaac come to the plantation yelling bout y'all niggers better do this and y'all niggers better do that and god damn it if you don't then y'all niggers better watch out!' Fact is, before everything was said and done, he was the one who needed to watch out.

The men the soldiers took told us how they and other slaves were beaten, kicked and spit on just because white people wanted to do these things to them. They treat a dog better then they treat a slave. And now they got them nightriders that catch you and beat you or even worse. They can do whatever they want to do to you and no law will help you because they is the law. I feels safe on this here plantation. And if I was to leave, what would I do? Farming and brick making is what I know, it's all I ever did. It's what my daddy did and his daddy before him and his daddy before him. So what would I do? I don't have no land. All I gots is these pants and this shirt on my back, these old boots on my feet, and even if I left, there would be a whole lot of road in front of me that I don't know nothing about. They say I can walk down it now, because they say I'm free. What's down that road is a fearful mystery but what's here on this plantation is people and things I know somethin' about.

Master Jones been good to me and mine, better than most masters I done heard about, so I don't knows if I wants to be free and don't even know what free is. To me it is just some fancy word that white folks made up to get us off this here plantation so they can kill us. Or do they just want us to leave our homes so they can give them to somebody else? A lot of white folks done lost everything because of the war, and now they have nothing. They also say we can stay and work for money. We can work for anybody, anywhere we wants to. That don't make no kind'a sense, working for money, cause we ain't never had none and don't know nothin' bout it, wouldn't know what to do with it. Most likely we'd just give it right back to them.

So here I is sitting on this log, looking at the road that lead off this here plantation. Some people say that they stayin' here and gon work for Master Jones. Then again others say they leavin' here and headin' up North. Lord I don't know what to do. I wish my folks was here to tell me. First Mama got sick workin' in them rice fields, and then Daddy went to Savannah with a bunch'a other slaves and never came back alive. Both of them left me here to fend for myself, not knowin' what to do. Sure I gots Aunt Fran and my three little cousins, but they in the same boat just like me. They don't know what's to be doing either. Lord help me. Lord help us.

## ◆ CHAPTER 1 ◆

My name is Isaiah Jones. At the end of the War Between the States, I was fifteen years old and mostly on my own. This is my story or at least as much as I can remember. You see, now I'm seventy years old, thank the lord, and my remembrance ain't none too good now-a-days because I lived first through one war when I was a boy and just got finished living through another one they fought all over the world.

I'm not saying my remembrance is all bad but some things stand out more than others do. I'm just glad that I'm still alive, and surprised by that fact to tell you the truth, after all the hell my life has seen.

Don't get me wrong, there have been some bright moments, and I ain't one to complain. I had some right good years in my day, even though they never seemed to last as long as the other kind of years.

Some folks call me a hard man, but I don't think I am. I'm the way this old world made me, and some people have a little trouble with that. Well I can't help that and I sure won't be losing any sleep over it. All I can do is be me, Isaiah Jones from Woodloe Plantation in Savannah, Georgia. A man that worked hard all his life and did the best that he could with what he had. I don't know if I made all the right choices in life but I do know that I always tried to do right by everyone. At least I hope and pray that I did. Anyway, this is my story.

It was a chilly day in April 1865 when Master Jones called all the slaves to the big house. I was in the cane fields when I heard the cowbell ringing. I heard that bell ring many times before that day but something was different about this time. I remember thinking that I didn't have time to worry about whatever was going on because I had too much work to do, and I wanted to get most of it done by that evening. But like everybody else, I walked quickly towards the house, asking if anyone knew what this was about. We all knew that the master's son, Lew, was back home and people were saying the war was supposed to be over. So what now? What could it be?

We stood around and waited for everybody to gather in front of the house. Once everyone was there Master Jones started talking.

"I don't rightly know how to tell ya'll this but, you don't have to work for me no more. All of you are free. Free to either stay or go. It's up to you. If you want to stay you can. If you want to go no one is going to stop you. You're not my slaves anymore and I'm no longer your master. From now on, I'm Mister Jones to all of you." Then he looked around and said, "I thank you for the years and the service that you have given me. You all know that you all are like family to me, and through the years I tried to treat you all fairly."

With that said, he turned around and walked back

into the house. Some of us started cheering and jumping around, hollering, "We's free! We's free!" Others just stood there, unable to talk because we didn't know what to say. We looked at each other, trying to figure out what Master Jones meant when he said he was now "Mister Jones." We all had heard that the war was about freeing us. Only thing was, we didn't think it was ever really going to happen. But it had happened, and there we were.

I walked back to the cane field and went back to work. There was a lot to think about, and I did my best thinking when I was working. I heard someone say, "Look at that fool, he too dumb to know he don't have to work no more."

Some of the men and women quit working that very day and said they were never working in anybody's fields no more. Two men ran past me laughing and jumping until they reached the end of the field and disappeared, not carrying a single thing but what they had on their backs. I finished the work I wanted to get done early that evening and slowly walked toward my cabin. It was the cabin where my father, my mother and I had once lived together. Now I lived there alone. I couldn't help hoping sometimes that when I opened the door they would be standing there waiting for me. Sometimes I felt sad knowing they wouldn't be there but I didn't have time for sadness that day. I had too much else on my mind. I went behind the cabin, which I generally thought of as my little house, got some water from a big barrel used to catch rain water, and washed my face and hands. Back inside the house, I got a piece of beef jerky and some bread from the wooden box sitting on a shelf over the potbelly stove. Then I started a fire in the stove, and made myself a cup of tea. I like a good cup of tea with honey in it.

As the house began to get warm, I sat at the table eating and thinking. What would daddy do? What would be best for me? Daddy never told me what to do or what not to do. Instead, he'd say, "If I was you I would or I wouldn't do this or that." I could almost hear him speaking the words when someone knocked on the door. It was Aunt Fran, my mother's sister, and my three little cousins, Andrea, Will, and Brook. They all came in and had a seat at the table. Aunt Fran looked at me with a worried look on her face and asked, "What chu gonna do Isaiah?"

"I don't rightly know Aunt Fran. I'm thinkin' I gotta study on this thing for a while. What chu gonna do?"

She got quiet for a minute and looked at me with that same sad serious look that she had when daddy went off to Savannah. It was like she knew the minute he left that he wasn't coming back. That look scared me the first time I saw it and it scared me when we was sitting at that table.

"Well you the oldest man in this family now Isaiah. That mean it up to you to make the decision."

I hadn't expected to hear that. It gave me even more to think about. Aunt Fran was twice my age and the closest thing I had to a mama since my own died and now here she was telling me I had to make this big decision for the whole family about whether we should leave or stay when I couldn't even decide for myself.

She had been married but her husband and the father of her children went and got his self snake-bit by a cotton mouth water moccasin in the rice fields, then died about six months before the freedom came. His name was Calvin, and he had been a blacksmith. Why he was in the rice fields at the time that he was nobody knew. He was a tall, strong, dark skinned man, who seemed to always have a smile on his face when he talked to you. He always seemed to be happy and would help anybody. Just by talking with him, he made you feel good no matter how bad your day was. He just had a way about him. When he died I didn't think Aunt Fran would ever stop crying. She and the kids cried for what seemed like three months or better. Some folks said that Aunt Fran was going to cry herself to death in order to be with her husband. I believed that if she didn't have her kids, she might have done just that. Her oldest child, Andrea was only seven years old and her youngest Brook was two.

It was so sad, one of the saddest things I ever saw in my life, that is besides losing my own mama and daddy and also that time when Lew's half-brother Isaac (on his mama's side) beat Lew's half-brother Robert (on his daddy's side) almost to a bloody death. I was thirteen or fourteen when that happened and I'll never forget it as long as I live because it was the only time on Woodloe I ever knew about that anybody got a beatin' like that, so bad and bloody that folks said it didn't just scar up Robert's body but scarred up his mind and almost killed his soul.

So now all of a sudden here I had my aunt and her three children to worry about as well as myself. Aunt Fran left and I went to bed. However I didn't get much sleep that night. The sun came up and I watched as the light slowly filled my small room. I got up off my pallet, nothing more than some sacks stuffed with straw and hand-sewn quilts to tell you the truth, but to me it was my bed. By the time I got dressed and went outside, people who usually would have been working in the fields by now were standing around the yard talking. Then some started packing their things and preparing to leave.

Several folks had gone to Old Lizzy, the root woman for advice. Certain ones she told just to follow their hearts. Certain other ones she told to follow the North Star as far as they could and don't look back. As for her, she said, "I'm too old to call myself goin' someplace else. I been part of this land for as long as I can remember and this land is part of me."

Later that day, a group of men decided to have a meeting and talk about the best thing to do. I was one of the first to get to the meeting place down by the riverbank that was called Jones Creek. I didn't know why we always met on the riverbank, but that's the way it always was. I looked at the water where I had learned to swim as a child and remembered how my daddy and I went crabbing and fishing on this river. I stood there smiling to myself, thinking about the good times I had with my daddy. With my eyes closed, I took a deep breath. As the salt air filled my lungs I could almost hear my father's voice telling me stories he had heard as a child, as we fished and caught crabs. Then somebody called my name. When I opened my eyes, Miss Lizzy's son Solomon was standing there looking at me.

"Is you alright?" he asked.

"Yes, I was remembering my daddy."

Then I walked toward the crowd of gathering men. One of the older men always spoke first. That was the way of the folks on Woodloe Plantation. Most of my life that had been Old Jordan, but he had passed back around Christmas time. We still had Big Vernest though. He was one of the oldest and one of the wisest.

"It don't make no sense whatsoever leaving our homes and moving elsewhere," said Big Vernest. "We all know Master Jones—"

"Only he ain't 'master' no mo', he 'mister' now!"

"If he 'mister' or if he 'master' we know he would never cheat us when it came to money, which most'a y'all don't know nothin' about but which all us gon have to learn somethin' about. We can work for him and he'll do right by us."

"That's right fine," somebody said, "if that's all you wants but this is our chance to live our lives the way we see fit, not having to answer to no master ever again."

"Besides," added another, "they say the northern army gon give us all forty acres and a mule. So now we all got the chance to be land owners."

After that, something just hit me and I said, "Forty acres and a mule don't give you no seed to plant, or no food to put in you stomach while you doin' the plantin'. It doesn't give you no clothes on your back or no roof over your head. You can't eat, wear or live in no forty acres and no mule. And 'posing that mule gets sick then up and die on you. Now you the one got to be the mule workin' them forty acres."

"Well what you think about all this Solomon?" asked Big Vernest. "What you say we ought'a do?"

We all turned to look at Solomon. He bent down and grabbed a hand full of mud from the river bank, like his mind was somewhere else completely, then he straightened back up and said, "Mama done already spoke on that."

Then he walked away.

Everybody started talking at the same time. It was plain to see there was no easy way to figure this out. So I just walked away and went to where Mama and Daddy (or at least where some of their clothes and things) were buried. I always went there when I had more on my mind than I knew how to deal with.

I sat on the ground next to my mother's grave. It was quiet and peaceful there. Birds sang in the trees and crickets jumped through the grass. Lying on the ground, I looked up at the clouds, watching them gently float by. Soon, I fell asleep and dreamed I was talking with my father. He had been a big man, stood almost seven feet tall, but was as gentle as a soul could be. He taught me to always stand up straight, and to always look at a person's eyes when I came across them, only to do it real fast if the person was white. In my dream, I told him that I loved him and asked him what I should do. "If it was me," he answered, "I'd stay right here on Woodloe for about five years, save as much of that spendin' money as I could, then find myself a road headin' north so I could go somewhere and make a different kind of life for myself."

When I woke up, I found Aunt Fran and told her we would stay for five years and save our money. Then we would be able to move to the North. She agreed and told the children we were staying.

# ◆ CHAPTER 2 ◆

It was a sad time on Woodloe Plantation. By the end of that week after our used-to-be Master Jones announced we were free, almost half the slaves who used to live and work there had gone. People like the house slaves Ada and Enoch stayed. Robert got a piece of land from Master Jones out toward the end of the plantation and started building a school house. Everybody knew that was between him and his white daddy but the rest of us wasn't about to be that lucky.

       Those of us used-to-be slaves who stayed signed on with Mister Jones, who most'a the time I couldn't help calling Master Jones, and worked the fields same way we'd always done. Instead of calling us slaves, they started calling us "sharecroppers." That meant that we would work the fields like before, but then come harvest and selling time, we would all share the money. That is after Mister Jones figured out how much we owed him for the things we used during the times we were planting. Mister Jones who used to be Master Jones kept the money books, and everyone's name was in it. Whenever you needed clothes or shoes or food, he wrote it in that book. Half the time I don't think he wrote anything at all, but that was just his way. He was a good man.

All of this happened in the spring when the fields were full of cane that would need every good pair of hands available to cut it. Cutting would just be the first part. After squeezing the juice out of the cane, it would have to be boiled to make syrup. Some of that was used to make rum and some to make sugar. With over half our people gone, the ones that stayed would have twice the amount of work to do. In some ways, it would be even more work than that because a good cane crop could give you two or three harvests. That wasn't even counting the smaller vegetable crops we grew for our own food or the work it took to get the rice paddies ready for the next rice crop. So much work was too much for certain folks to even think about so they up and left too.

After all its years of productivity and prosperity, with so few people left to work the land, Woodloe Plantation was in big trouble. Something had to be done, but what? Those of us who stayed found ourselves working from sun up to sun down. We did that seven days a week and still the work never seemed to get done. If it wasn't for Robert leaving his schoolhouse to work some days and Lew pitching in to work just as long and hard as the rest of us, I probably would have just quit and moved on myself.

Then one morning I went to work and saw something I had never seen before. It was a whole bunch'a white folks working right alongside the black folks. We were used to seeing Lew in the fields every now and then because they was his fields belonging to him and his daddy, but these other white folks were something different. Come to find out, they had moved to Woodloe and were now living in the cabins left behind by the used-to-be slaves who left. It was a whole heap of them and it seemed to me that these white people were just about as poor as we were. Some of them had lost everything they had in the war and some of them were women with children that had lost their husbands in the war. Others never had anything to start with.

Still, most of them acted like they were better than us, or like they hated us because they figured that, somehow, we were the reason for them being poor. Some of them called us "niggras" or "darkies" like Isaac used to do, and more than once Lew had to remind them that we had names. Some of them he had to run off the plantation altogether. They weren't going to let no ex-slaves tell them what to do or how to do it. And then some of them was just hard working people trying to survive the war and get on with their lives like the rest of us. They worked just as long and hard as everybody else and never complained. Before that day, I'd always thought all white people were rich like Mister Jones.

# ♦ CHAPTER 3 ♦

Somehow we made it through the growing season. We harvested the cane and made barrels of syrup and rum like we'd always done. By the time we come close to finishing with one crop, workers started getting ready for another. Soon it was the middle of summer. Ditches had to be cleaned and dug to route the water to and from the rice fields.

This work was hard and backbreaking, but with the new workers that came along, we could take Saturday and Sunday time off to get some rest if we wanted to. Rest was something that agreed with me and I was sleeping real fine one Sunday morning when I dreamed I saw my daddy sitting up in a tree filled with all different kinds of fruit. When I called to him, he didn't answer, so I climbed up the tree to see what he was doing. In his hands, he had a big book. It was so big I didn't think I'd be able to hold it when he held it out but I did. Then it started getting real light. It got so light it started rising up on the air and lifted me right along with it. Then I woke up and knew I needed to find out exactly where Robert's school was so I could learn whatever books had to teach me. I started going to the school at night. A lot of the older people started going too, black folks and white folks. We learned how to read, write, and also how to speak. That's right, speak! I'll never forget the first time Robert showed me my name in writing: I-S-A-I-A-H. I used to write it by making a mark like this: -+-. But never again. I was proud as I could be when I wrote it myself and didn't have to make a mark anymore.

Next I learned how to count money. This was important because I was going to be making some. Robert told us a story once about how he almost got himself in trouble when he and Mister Jones went to the general store. He almost let on that he knew how to count money. I knew that Master Jones wouldn't cheat us, but I just wanted to be sure about what I made and what I spent. I knew that we would be leaving in five years and I had to save as much as I could. Aunt Fran and my little cousins were depending on me. With this in mind I would do whatever it took to make it.

After our first year, Fran and I had fifty-three dollars. We figured that after five years we would have over four hundred dollars. If the children worked we would have even more, but in the meantime they were still a bit too young to work. At the age of seven, Andrea was old enough to work, but she had to stay home and keep an eye on her little brothers, Will and Brook, which in fact was a job itself.

Andrea was a pretty girl with long plaits hanging from both sides of her head, slender, and with beautiful dark skin like her father's. She even had his smile. She was a smart girl and just like her mother she always seemed to be working at home, staying busy doing this and that. She loved to talk and would do so with anyone who would stop and give her a moment of their time. If she wanted to know something, no matter what it was, she would ask about it. Then once she heard the answer she would never forget it. I swear that girl knew the first words she ever heard and could repeat them just like they were spoken. Between her big smile and all the questions she would ask, if she ever stopped you to talk, you knew that you would be there awhile. Except for that it was alright because everyone loved her and were all too happy to spend the time with her when they could.

Will was a skinny five-year-old who was always getting into something. He was the spitting image of his father, walked and talked just like him. With his kind and gentle spirit, and striking resemblance to his father, I always believed he was Fran's favorite. He seemed to always want to know about making things and would grab at different objects like tools and clothes, one of those children who picked up on things quickly. From sun up to sun down he was always moving, so full of energy with plenty to spare. I don't believe that boy could keep still for five minutes or else it would kill him dead. That's just the way he was.

Aunt Fran said I had been like that at his age, but I didn't recollect being his age. All I know is that I hoped that he would calm down someday because he just flat wore you out.   Fran or Andrea had to keep an eye on him at all times.

Brook was a fat little two-year-old. With his round face and big brown eyes, he looked more like Aunt Fran and my mother. I called him my little big head cousin. He was quiet and seemed to be a happy child, always trying to help with the work around the house despite the fact that he was too little to do much of anything except get in the way. Aunt Fran made a small broom for him and would let him sweep the floor with it so he would feel like he was helping. Of course he couldn't do much of anything, but that didn't stop him from trying. He was happy thinking he was doing it.  When he was done he would ask, "I do good?" We would hug him and say, "You sure did Brook, you done real good."

# ♦ CHAPTER 4 ♦

One Sunday, some of the men who had been there before
said they were going to Savannah and asked if I wanted to
go with them. I had never been anywhere, except right
there on Woodloe, but I knew that sooner or later I would
have to leave. So I said "Yes" and hopped in the back of
the wagon, one of the same wagons that for years had
carried the cane from the fields to the cane grinder and rice
to the rice mill.

I was on it heading away from the plantation, away
from my home, for the very first time. I began to feel kind
of sick as the wagon slowly rolled down the long dirt road
and through the arched gate that led off the plantation.

We turned to the left and headed down another dirt
road. There were wooden houses on this road, nice houses.
One of the men said that Negro people owned these houses.
I didn't believe him until I saw some children playing in
the yards. Then I knew it was true. They had their own land
and their own houses. We rode on and I saw big houses
with fancy yards and gardens. I asked one of the men if

Negro people owned them too. Everybody started laughing, so I laughed with them.

We can only wish we owned something like that," one of the men said.

I thought to myself that one day I would own something like that.

We passed several Negro soldiers wearing the same blue uniforms with gold buttons that white Union soldiers wore. They smiled and nodded towards us and we waved back. The sick feeling I'd had went away. I stared at all the fancy houses. Everywhere I looked, there were Negroes and White People walking around doing whatever they felt like doing. Some of them looked really bad, dirty from head to toe. They appeared to be hungry, men, women and children begging for anything someone would give them. I felt sorry for them and couldn't help thinking that if Fran and I had left Woodloe, we too might be in their shoes.

The wagon pulled in front of the general store and stopped. The men got out of the wagon and headed towards the store. I stayed in it looking at all the buildings and the people around me. A lot of those giant fancy buildings made the big house on Woodloe look like one of the little houses on the plantation. I had never seen anything like it in my life. I even saw Negro people wearing fancy clothes like the white people wore. I knew those people didn't work in anybody's field. Not dressed the way they were dressed. What did they do for a living? How were they able to dress the way they did and walk around like they had all the time in the world to do nothing but look pretty?

One black man wearing a tan-colored suit with a vest and a watch on a gold chain hanging out his breast pocket came walking towards the wagon. I got up the nerve to ask him, "Sir, you mind if I ask what you do to earn your pay?"

"I own a juke joint," he said, stopping and smiling.

"A juke joint? What's a juke joint?"

He looked at me sitting on the back of that wagon and laughed.

"You fresh off the plantation boy ain't you?"

"I guess, me and some of the fellas just come from Woodloe. I been livin' and workin' there all my life."

"Oh I'm sure you have. Well a juke joint is someplace people go to forget all about working. It' where they dance, drink and have a good time. They get a chance to spend some'a that money they work so hard to get. I provide 'em with some real pleasurable times at Joe's Place and they pay me accordingly. That's how come I'm able to dress in this fine suit that you can't take your eyes off."

"Yessir, ok, you have a good day."

He smiled, laughed again, and then kept on walking.

It wasn't just Negro men that had on fancy clothes. Some of them women had on dresses just like the ones Mrs. Jones used to wear when she felt like sitting on the porch and drinking tea or lemonade all day. Some of them had these pretty round things on a stick that stopped the sun from shining on their heads. Some even wore fancy hats and gloves. It was a sight to behold, yes lord a sight to behold.

Then something happened. I noticed the looks on the faces of many of the white folks. They didn't seem too happy at all to see me sitting there on that wagon looking at them. They had what my daddy called, "pig eyes." That was when I got scared and remembered what daddy had said about not looking directly at white folks for too long. I stopped studying them and sat there looking down at the ground.

After a while, the men came back from inside the store. One of them asked me why I hadn't come inside. I told him I hadn't brought any money with me.

"You could'a come in anyway just to look around. Peoples do it all the time."

They piled back onto the wagon, put the things they'd bought in a box on the back of it, and we headed down the road. I told them about the man I had met and what he said about his juke joint.

"Oh you met Joe," said the driver. "We're on our way to his joint right now to have some fun."

Joe had said that people who went to his place had their fun by dancing, drinking, and having some 'real pleasurable times.' For me, a good time usually meant a third helping of one of Aunt Fran's special Sunday dinners but something told me this juke joint thing was going to be very different. On our way there, I took another look around at the people walking the streets of Savannah. I saw more of them that were in mighty bad shape. They had nothing. I saw a heap of folks just begging with hardly any clothes on their backs. They were both Whites and Negroes alike, begging for food, money, or anything somebody would give them. But I didn't see anybody helping them. Not the towns-people or the soldiers. If I'd had anything I would have given it to them. I started feeling sick again.

We headed back toward the plantation then turned off the main road and down a long narrow dirt road with a ditch along the side of it. About two miles down the road we came to a clearing where I saw a big wooden house in the middle of a field. There were wagons, horses and mules all around it. I saw people standing around outside and I heard music playing inside. I remember thinking that this is what some people do on Sundays. The wagon pulled in front of the juke joint and the men jumped out, then ran in the front door where some women were waiting and hugged them. They didn't care about the mule or the wagon.

They ran and laughed like little children. I didn't understand it. Some people walking around looked sick, like they could barely stand up, and some others were asleep on the ground beneath a tree. I even saw one man looking through the pockets of another man sleeping on the ground. It didn't bother him one bit that I was looking right at him. I wondered what kind of place this was that made grown people act the way these people were acting.

I got out the wagon, slowly walked over to the front door, and looked inside. There had to be over a hundred people around this place. Inside the juke joint was a big smoky room with foul smelling air. Tables and chairs sat in the middle of the room and all along three walls. A long counter sat in front of the fourth wall next to a back door. A group of four men played music at the other end of the room. People drank scrap iron alcohol, gin, and plum wine, played cards, laughed, cussed, and danced everywhere I looked. Some of those tables where the men played cards had piles of money that they passed back forth like it didn't mean nothing at all.

One lady sold fish and chicken dinners that she cooked outside the back door. Some people were asleep at the tables. Women were dancing wildly with some of the men and even sitting on some of their laps. I knew right then and there that this was no place for me. I turned around and quickly headed back to the wagon. One of the men from Woodloe called my name, but I acted like I didn't hear him and decided to walk back home. This just wasn't a place where I wanted to be.

As I walked down the road leading away from the juke joint, I saw a lady coming towards me. She was one of the best looking women I had ever seen in my life, with big brown eyes, long black hair, and a smile that could warm your soul on the coldest day in winter. It was hard not to stare at her. Seem like we stopped walking at the same time.

"A handsome man like you shouldn't be walking all by hisself on a beautiful day like this," she said. "What's your name?"

"Name's Isaiah."

"Well Mr. Isaiah you can call me Miss Lilith," she said, and smiled real big. "Suppose we turn back around and keep each other company while you buy me a drink."

"Well, um, I sure wouldn't mind buyin' you somethin' to drink seeing how you're so thirsty and everything Miss Lilith but my daddy always told me to tell the truth and the truth is I ain't got no money. See, me and Aunt Fran—"

"I don't need to hear no no-count nigger tellin' me some no-count story."

Her face didn't look so pretty when she said those words then threw her head back and walked on pass me. That was the first time in my life anyone talked directly that way to me. Her words hurt because I never thought of myself as no-count. I decided not to walk home after all.

That woman had made me upset. I felt like someone had hit me in my gut. She didn't even know me, still she was calling me that. She might have been pretty on the outside, but she was sure enough ugly on the inside. I turned around and went back to the wagon, then sat in the back of it looking at all them fools and waiting for the men to come out of the juke joint.

It was almost dusk dark, about four hours later when they finally came back to the wagon. None of them were in any shape to drive it so I did. As we went down the dirt road I saw another wagon that someone had driven into a ditch. They must have hopped on the horse or mule and rode on off. It looked like one of the wheels was broken. I thought to myself that if I had let one of them fools hold the reins, the same thing might have happened to us. Besides we had to take good care of that wagon because it didn't belong to any of us. It was Mister Jones' and he was nice enough to let us use it from time to time. I remembered mama and daddy telling me not to call people fools, but if that shoe fit you wear it. I couldn't have juke joint foolishness in my life because Aunt Fran and her children were depending on me.

The darker it got the more scared I became. I had heard about them night-riders that went around looking for Negroes to terrorize and beat on. This was some white folks' way of having fun. I jumped every time I heard anything move, and I swore that I would never get myself in any mess like that again.

With the moon nowhere in sight, it was pitch dark when we got back to Woodloe. All the men in the back of the wagon were asleep, and had been for some time. When I woke them up, they all got out the wagon and just walked away. Not one stayed to help me unhitch the mule and put him in the barn. Then I went home and fixed myself a bite to eat before going to bed.

I must have been more tired than I realized because soon as I went to bed, I fell asleep and dreamed I was back on the road walking away from the juke joint when I saw that pretty lady who said she was thirsty and called herself Miss Lilith. Only this time another woman was walking beside her. When they got closer, the second woman whispered something in Miss Lilith's ear. She stopped and lowered her eyes, bowed just a little bit, and said, "Good afternoon kind sir." Then I heard my daddy's voice say, "Tell her 'Yes Ma'am, a fine afternoon indeed.' So I said what he'd told me to. It wasn't until the women walked on by that the second one turned around and I saw she had the same face as my mama. Seem like tears rushed up from my heart to my eyes and I wanted to call her back but everything just faded until I slept deeper and harder.

The next day while we were working, some of the men who had gone to the juke joint looked sick and a couple of them threw up right there in the field. One didn't show up for work at all that day. Still they talked about how much fun they'd had and said they were going back next Sunday. That was the kind of fun I didn't need or want. They all had wasted their money and had nothing to show for it. Except for what they had brought from the store before they went to that juke joint. Lucky for them they'd had the foresight to go to the store and buy the things they needed first.

Now I knew how that man named Joe was able to wear his fancy clothes. He had a place where people had fun spending their money. That whole thing gave me an idea. Aunt Fran could cook these men some breakfast and supper from Monday to Friday and charge each of them a dollar each week. That way at least they would eat some good food during the week before giving up all their money on the weekend and at the same help us save up to go north. Fran thought this was a good idea and didn't waste no time getting started.

# ♦ CHAPTER 5 ♦

After my first Sunday visit to the juke joint, I didn't want to go back in town for a while. Later in the week, I told Fran and the kids what I saw. Their eyes filled with excitement and they all laughed at the part about the woman calling me no-count. They couldn't wait to go into Savannah. I told them I'd get the wagon and we'd all go one day but I didn't know when. Like I said, it would be a while. Besides, we had to save our money and we had too much work to do. That meant we didn't have time to waste.

Now that I had seen how some other Negro people were living, I couldn't stop thinking that one day I would be living better than I was now. Soon Mister Jones told us that we could all earn more money on a more regular basis if we worked by the day and worked six or seven days a week. I think he pretty much had to do it that way because some people were leaving and some people were passing through all the time, which meant they weren't willing to stick around waiting until harvest time before getting paid. Since it got more and more hard for him to keep a whole lot of people working the fields on a permanent kind of basis, he started paying some by the day, some by the week, and some by the month. He said we didn't have to but if we worked extra days then he would pay us extra for those days.

Most folks at Woodloe just worked five days a week from Monday until Friday, then got what they earned. Fran and I generally worked every day of the week for the next three months. Lots of times folks would come to us and try to borrow our money after spending theirs, but we always told them no. Then they would have the gall to get mad at us about it. We worked too hard for that money and we were not about to just give it away.

July rolled around and the days got long and hot. The work in the rice fields was hard and treacherous, not to mention dangerous. Snakes were really bad that year. It seemed like somebody would kill one every day. Mister Lew stopped working in the rice fields altogether. He didn't say why, but I think it was because he was scared of snakes. I remember hearing a story about how Robert kept him from getting bit by a snake when they were boys. Not many of the other white folks would work in the rice fields. Something would make them sick with fever. Folks say it was from the mosquito bites. I couldn't see how a little old skeeter could make anybody sick. They'd been biting me all my life and I ain't never got sick from it.

Some days I didn't think Fran would make it working in them fields. I think she became afraid of snakes after her husband Calvin got bit by one and died. But she was a strong woman. Fear or no fear, she kept right on going to the fields every day. She said she had dreamed that her children would go to school in the north and become something more than a field hand or a house Negro. In the meantime, they started going to Robert's little schoolhouse in the daytime just like I went sometimes at night. Robert taught us a lot of things, he was one smart man. Sometimes I'd see him leaving the big house with his arms full of books and other times I'd see him bring books to the house. Him, Mister Jones, and Mister Lew would sit on the porch some Sundays in bright daylight passing books back and forth and talking about them.

Me and Fran worked on, trying not to spend any money and saving every penny that we could. Neither of us bought any new clothes or much of anything else that year. We were a raggedy bunch, but we kept our rags clean. Still, we did take the children to town that December and got them some new clothes. I can remember the look on their faces when we told them they were going to Savannah.

They all started jumping around and acting crazy. I didn't blame them one bit because I remembered how I felt when I first went to town. I got the mule from the barn and hitched up the wagon, then drove to Aunt Fran's cabin and called for everyone to come on out. Brook and Will came running through the door right away and jumped on the back of the wagon.

However, Aunt Fran and Andrea seemed to need some more time.

"Why don't we leave them here and just us men go to town," said Will.

"Us men? What man you see in this wagon besides me?"

I had to laugh when he said it. He knew I never did cotton to waiting on anyone for very long unless something else was going on to hold my attention. But I wasn't about to leave them because I would have never heard the last of it. So we waited.

When we finally drove through the plantation gate, Brook stood up in the back of the wagon and shouted, "WOO WEE!" That big headed boy scared me so bad that I pulled back on the reigns to stop the mule and he fell right off the wagon. When he stood up he was covered with dust from head to toe. We all laughed and I couldn't stop until water started coming from my eyes. I can see Brook now standing there covered from head to toe with dust. That boy was a hand full.

When we got to Savannah, the children wanted to go running off in every direction at once. Before they got off the wagon I told them not to look white folks in the eyes since they seemed to get mad if they caught you looking directly at them. It took some doing just trying to keep up with them children. At one point, Will wandered off and we couldn't find him. From the look in Fran's eyes, she was sure that something bad had happened to him. When I found him he was in the blacksmith's shop telling the blacksmith, an elderly Negro man named James, the best way to hold a horseshoe so he could hit it just right to make a better fit for the horse. I apologized to the blacksmith for the boy bothering him and told Will he didn't know what he was talking about, "So stop bothering folks."

To my surprise, the Blacksmith said Will did know what he was talking about and that his idea was a good one. Hush my mouth! I guess you never know what children do and don't know. Those children were a lot smarter than I was at their age, but then again I wasn't allowed to read or write when I was their age.

Me and Will found the others again and we all went to the general store. Fran and I bought the children some brand new clothes, shoes, and some rock candy, then we all headed back to the plantation. Once we got back to Woodloe, Fran and the children went into their house. Brook wanted to help me with the mule, but I told him that I could do it by myself. It made me think about the last time I had gone to Savannah and come back with a wagon full of drunken men. Then I went to the graveyard to talk with my parents. It was a cool night with a breeze coming off the river and the air was filled with the smell of salt. After about an hour or two I walked home and went to bed.

Those children sure loved that trip to Savannah, and talked about all the people with their own houses and fancy clothes. One day, Will asked Aunt Fran why we didn't live like the people he saw. I think he was embarrassed because of the clothes Fran and I had on. They were a bit worn but we kept them clean. I could see the sadness in her eyes as she told him that one day we would live like that. Fran told him that sometimes you have to make do with what you have until you can get what you want. She told all the kids that if they worked hard and saved their money, one day they too would live like the people they saw in Savannah. Maybe even better than them.

That was our plan. It was the reason Fran and I worked so long and so hard. And I knew in my heart that we were going to make it off of that plantation one day. I wouldn't have it any other way. I would have to die before I gave up.

# ♦ CHAPTER 6 ♦

Another year came and went. It was February and we had been free for over two years. To me there wasn't much difference between being free and being a slave. The cold was just as cold in the winter time and the sun was just as hot in the summer. In fact, now that most of the folks had gone from Woodloe plantation, the work there was much harder.

Oh yeah, we did have them white folks working with us from time to time and acting like they knew more about farming than anyone else. I guess that was one of the reasons I never became friends with any of them. Fran and the kids did, but not me. I just didn't trust them. It was like my mother use to say, "Either your soul agrees with somebody or it don't."

Except for that I couldn't tell much difference. Sometimes, back then, I couldn't help but think we were better off the way we were when we were slaves. When Mister Jones was Master Jones, he used to give us our food and clothes, but when he became Mister Jones, we had to buy our food and clothes with the money he gave us for working. Seemed like I had a heap more worries than when we weren't free. I just went to work, did what I had to do, then came home. When I needed something, Master gave it to me and I was happy with that.

But then I had to spend my time thinking about things I ain't never had and about going places I had never been while at the same time trying to save money to do them both. Yeah, I thought we might have been better off before all that freedom stuff happened. Then years later I realized that being free or not being free wasn't the real problem for me. It was the fact that freedom came after mama and daddy had both gone to glory and wasn't there to share it with us. Freedom would have meant a whole lot more if slavery hadn't already taken their lives.

On top of everything else, I worried about the money we'd been saving. Folks knew we'd been working extra days and saving our money. They also knew I didn't go to town and give it away, and that Fran and I didn't buy anything unless we really had to. I hid the money in a clay jar and put it in a hole under the wood-burning stove, afraid someone might just up and steal it. I didn't know what I would do if that happened.

We still thought about finding work for Andrea. She would turn nine that year and Will would turn seven, which meant Will could keep an eye on Brook while Andrea worked. She could cook and clean or do the clothes washing. That would give us a little more money come the next year. Maybe she would work in the fields with us. She had been wanting to work in the fields all the while now, but Fran said it was too dangerous because of them snakes and such. When there were more folks around, we had adults looking out for the children while we worked. Or some parents just had their children working right along side them, like mine had me from about the time I was maybe four or five. Then it just got too dangerous for the little ones.

House work would be the best thing for her. Maybe Miss Ada could use some help in the big house; that would be good. I'd heard tell that Miss Ada wasn't much older than Andrea when she first started working in the big house. Andrea could cook everything her mother could cook and there was no one better at cleaning than her.

From time to time she and the boys came over to my house and cleaned up. I must say they did a pretty good job at it. I never did do much cleaning, other than washing my clothes and the dishes. Besides there wasn't anybody but me in the house. They seemed to enjoy coming to their older cousin's house to clean up and make me laugh. Half the time we would sit around and I would tell them stories that my father and Old Jordan had told me. As I told the stories, excitement would fill their faces and sometimes they'd grab onto each other for protection, as if the story was real and they were in some kind of danger. Once I had finished telling one story, they never failed to ask for another. Sometimes I'd go ahead and tell it and sometimes I wouldn't. Fact is, that was the only time Will would sit still. I enjoyed spending time with them children. This was one of their favorite stories, called *Boshama the King*:

Boshama (Ba-she-Ma) was a proud warrior with many cattle and many wives. He had fought in a lot of wars but was never harmed. Some said he was a child of the spirits because no harm could come to him. Boshama said it was because he studied his enemy before he fought them.

One day, after all the wars had been fought and won, peace came to his land. All the tribes were now living in peace. Now Boshama had time to hunt and enjoy his very large family. He didn't know just how many children he had because most of the time when they were born he was off somewhere fighting. Then one day Boshama decided it was time to count his children. He called his many wives together and told them to bring all of his children to him. One by one they came to him and called him father; as they knelt down in front of him. Boshama counted twenty-two children which made him even more proud than he already was. He was a happy man.

Being a good warrior also made Boshama a good hunter. While hunting one day for food, he heard strange sounds coming from deep in the jungle. As he got closer to the sounds he saw strange people, with skin of many colors, who when they talked made sounds that he didn't understand. They were dressed in garments of a kind he had never seen and they carried weapons unlike any he knew of. Boshama never let them know that he was watching them. He stayed hidden and watched as they moved though the jungle, killing all that they came in contact with. He watched them as they made camp and he watched them as they slept. Boshama being a warrior could have killed them in their sleep but he didn't.

After watching these strange men for two days, Boshama saw them go into one of the neighboring villages and capture all the people. He saw them kill the king and beat the men, women and children and tie them up. Boshama knew the people of this tribe and he knew that they were not at war with any other tribes. He asked himself why these strange men had done this terrible thing. Boshama decided to help these people and kill these strange men. Boshama stayed hidden in the jungle watching and waiting. He studied them and waited for his chance to free the people of this tribe and kill the strange men who had done this awful thing to them.

That night Boshama called on the spirits of his ancestors for strength. He went down to the river's edge and covered his body with mud from the river, and then he rolled around in some leaves, letting them stick to the mud. Afterwards, he slowly crawled into the camp of the strangers. He moved ever so slowly for he knew that patience was a warrior's greatest weapon. Without making a sound, one at a time, he killed all of them except for one. When the sun came up, the one that he had left alive saw what had taken place that night and ran off screaming that the jungle had killed his friends. Boshama returned to the river to wash the mud from his body and thanked his ancestors.

The people of the village were amazed by the fact that Boshama alone had freed them. He told them to gather all their belongings and move their village someplace else. They told him that their king had been killed and since he had killed the ones that killed the king, he should be their king now. They said they needed a leader because and without a king they were all doomed. Boshama thought about this for awhile then said that he would be their king. He named his new tribe of people Dewasi (Da-Wa-see), then went to his own village to get his wives and children. He told the people of his village what had happened and how he had killed all the strange men, which he called Tobob (Two-bob). Boshama knew that more Tobob would soon be coming. He didn't know when but he knew that sooner or later more would come. So Boshama and his wives and all of his children along with his new tribe went deep into the jungle where the Tobob would never find them.

Boshama lived to be an old man and fathered forty-one children. He taught his sons patience, and how to fight and hunt as he watched all of his children grow. His tribe became strong and their numbers increased. They never went back to the place where they had seen the Tobob and they never saw any others in their lifetime. As time passed, his tribe did hear stories of how Tobob captured the people of other tribes and they were never heard from again

# ♦ CHAPTER 7 ♦

Aunt Fran said I needed to find somebody and think about starting a family. I told her that she and the kids were all the family I needed for the time being. Maybe once we left and started over in the North, I would find someone. She didn't pay me any mind and one Sunday morning she came walking across the yard over to my house with this lady while I was taking it easy sitting outside.

"This here Miss Bonnie," Fran said, "and this here Isaiah."

"Pleased to meet you," I said as I stood up.

She was one pretty lady, tall and slender with skin that looked smooth like a baby's, black curly hair down to her shoulders, big brown eyes, and dimples. Did I say she was pretty? She was way more than that, she was *downright* pretty. I stood there smiling like some fool with half a brain in his head. How long I stood there just looking at her and smiling I don't know.

"Boy where's your manners, ain't you going to invite us in?" asked Fran.

I felt all warm and funny inside. I had never felt like that before. Was I in love with this lady that I had just met? Bonnie, I even liked the sound of her name. Fran said that Bonnie was from a plantation a ways down the road called Sheffield. She didn't have any family left there. They had all taken off as soon they were freed, didn't make any plans or anything, just started screaming happy and running. Bonnie was working and saving her money the same way that Fran and I were.

Fran said they had met at a Sunday go to meeting church thing about three months before. Since then they had become good friends. Bonnie and I were about the same age and I knew that I was in big trouble. The kind of trouble you get into when you listen with your heart. I ain't never had no lady friend or nothing like that. So at the time I didn't know what to do or say, or even how to act. I felt like running out the door, jumping and shouting at the top of my voice, but I didn't.

We all sat there and talked for a good long time. Well Fran and Bonnie did most of the talking and I sat there with this big dumb smile on my face and listened. Soon they both got up and headed to the door. I remember walking behind them with that big smile on my face. I stood at the door and watched as they both walked across the yard and they went into Fran's house. I hit myself on the head when I remembered that I didn't even say goodbye or anything.

I went back in my house and sat at the table. I could still smell Bonnie in the house. I remember saying to myself, *I don't need this, and it's not a part of my plans.* Shortly afterwards, I went to bed. That night I kept seeing Bonnie's face and hearing her voice, and I could still smell her. I didn't know what was happening to me, but I didn't like it.

The next morning I got out of bed and went to the fields to work. Fran was already working when I got there. I asked her where Bonnie was, and she told me that she had gone back home last night. I said, "Oh well," and started to work. I tried to play like it didn't make no difference to me, but I couldn't stop thinking about Bonnie. I wondered if she had made it home safely. I had to see her again, so I decided to go to the next Sunday meeting thing. I knew she would be there. I wasn't going to hear no preacher talk about no kingdom come like they do sometimes down by the river. I was going to see Bonnie. So I told Fran I would go with her and the kids on the next Sunday. A big smile came across her face.

"'Bout high time you be getting some religion," she said.

I had better sense than to tell her it wasn't religion I wanted but Bonnie.

The next Sunday morning I woke early, washed off, and got dressed in my best clothes. They weren't much better than the rest of my clothes, but they were clean. Then I went to Fran's house. As I walked across the yard I could smell Miss Ada's biscuits cooking in the big house. The smell made me realize I hadn't eaten anything, but I wasn't hungry. Fran and the kids weren't quite ready yet so I waited in the yard. I felt happy as I thought I should really be in the fields earning some extra pay, but here I was chasing after this lady that I didn't even know.

Fran and the kids eventually came out of the house and we all walked to the church, which was almost halfway between the plantation and Savannah. When we got there I saw a lot of people. It was funny to me to hear them call each other "Sister Somebody" or "Brother So-and-so." I didn't understand that one. Maybe it was because I didn't have no sisters or brothers that I wasn't inclined to start calling people I didn't know sister or brother. At least not just because some preacher said so.

Then I saw her walking towards the church with a beautiful smile on her face. Even from a distance she made me feel weak, warm, and all funny inside. I wanted to run over to her and just hug her. Needless to say I didn't do that. I just said to myself, "Lord have mercy!" and acted like I didn't see her.

She walked over to where Fran and I were.

"Hello," she said.

Boy did I love her smile and her voice. She and Fran hugged.

"Nice day we having," I said.

I don't know why I didn't hug her. I wanted to but I didn't. Each of the kids gave her a hug. Then we all walked inside the church. We had a seat on a hard wooden bench and listened to the preacher who talked too long. All this sitting made my hind parts hurt, and my stomach started making noise. Then that preacher started asking for folks to give him money. He called it a poor-cent. Fran and the children all gave him a nickel. I was kind of upset about this because we worked hard for that money and they just gave it to this man for talking to them and making them sit on hard benches. Boy was I glad when that preacher stopped all his talking and church was over. All I could think about was Bonnie, and how hungry I was. After we got out of that hot church I asked Bonnie if I could walk her home.

"I would be very happy if you did," she said with a smile.

I wanted to jump for joy, but I didn't. I was the perfect southern gentleman as we talked and walked together. Before I knew it we were at the Sheffield Plantation where Bonnie lived. She asked me if I wanted to go to her house and I told her no, maybe later, and that I'd best be getting along. Then I asked her if I could come courting next week Saturday.
Bonnie laughed and said, "You didn't come to church to hear no preacher today, did you?"

I just smiled.

"Well, then I guess I'd be one proud and lucky young woman to have you come courting next week Saturday."

I took her by the hand, gently squeezed it, and said goodbye. Bonnie hugged my neck, then turned and walked away. I stood there looking like somebody had just hit me up side my head with a stick. Bonnie even looked good as she was walking away. Yes I was in love for the first time in my life. I sang and smiled nearly all the way back to Woodloe Plantation. Then I remembered that I hadn't found out what house Bonnie lived in and I hadn't told her what time I would be coming over. That was dumb of me but I guess that's what love will do to you. You can't think right when you find yourself in love. You even do things that you wouldn't do at any other time, like walking down a road and singing at the top of your voice. White folks could have heard me and killed me. Thinking back on it, it was a fool thing to do, but going from one plantation to another, just like traveling to Savannah, was all new to me.

The week went by slowly, and I thought of Bonnie as the days dragged out. I worked some extra hours and went a couple times to Robert's week-night school just to fill up the time and make it pass quicker. Finally, Saturday morning arrived. I woke up and fixed myself breakfast. Yep, I had learned my lesson about not eating before I went somewhere. That morning I ate grits with crabmeat, one of Miss Ada's biscuits and some tea. I knew there was no way I was going to be working that day. I had Bonnie on the brain and couldn't get her off.

About seven o'clock I walked over to Fran's house. I told her I would be calling on Bonnie that day. From the way she started jumping around and screaming, you would have thought somebody had stuck a burning stick to her.

"I'm so glad for you," she screamed. "You two are going to be so good together." I only wish your mother was here to see you courting. She would be so proud of you."

"Actually, I don't know nothin' about courting," I said.

"No Isaiah I guess you don't."

"What's the best time to call on a lady?"

"Noon is a good and proper time. That way you can have lunch together and can't nobody say you sneakin' around doin' stuff you shouldn't ought'a be doin'."

Since it was just after seven o'clock, I had four hours before I could go see Bonnie. It would take less than a half hour to walk to her plantation, which left three and a half hours to wait.

The time passed so slowly but I finally got to Sheffield Plantation. As I walked near a row of houses, I saw two elderly ladies sitting outside one of them. Both of them puffed on a pipe and eyed me like I was a fox sniffing around a hen house.

"Hello," I said, "could I trouble y'all to tell me where Miss Bonnie live?"

"Oh you must be Isaiah."

They laughed, and then said something about me being good looking. I wasn't sure what they meant by that.

"Not being disrespectful but can you tell me where Miss Bonnie live or not?"

They pointed at the same time to the house across the yard.

"Thank you," I said, and walked towards the house.

Bonnie's house had flowers planted in the front of it and pretty cloth hanging in the windows. I walked up to the door and knocked on it.

"Who is it?" came Bonnie's soft voice from the other side.

"Me," I said, "Me, Isaiah, Miss Bonnie."

The door slowly opened and I saw her face, that big smile and those pretty dimples.

"Come in," she said, "have a seat."

Once I was inside, she leaned out the door and waved at the two old women sitting on the porch, then closed it.

I was as nervous as a long tailed cat in a room full of rocking chairs. Bonnie's house was a far cry better than my cabin. It was the same one room kind of house, but she had flowers in jars and the whole place smelled sweet like her. She must have known that I was nervous because she said we didn't have to stay in the house.

"Let's go for a walk around the plantation."

I didn't know what was wrong with me. I guess being alone with Bonnie for the first time in my life was a bit too much. I jumped up from the chair that I was sitting in and opened the door. Bonnie walked out ahead of me and I closed the door behind us. In my day, when a young man went to courting, someone older was always around to keep an eye on what was going on. But since Bonnie's folks were both gone and her other family had left the plantation, we were on our own. Maybe that's why I was so nervous. It didn't feel right being alone in the house with her. It just didn't sit right with me. It must not have sat right with those two old women either because they had moved off the porch and were standing in the yard looking right at the door when we opened it to come out. Bonnie yelled "Hey," and waved.

As we walked, Bonnie showed me around and told me about the plantation. She told me that she was an only child and that she had lost her parents the same way I had. However, she had a lot of aunts and uncles that helped to raise her. She said they all left the plantation just as soon as they could. Shortly after that, she met Fran at church and found out what we were doing, so she decided to stay and try to save her money. Then she would leave when she had enough money to start over somewhere else.

We had been walking and talking for a while, and then I felt good and ready to go back to Bonnie's house and get something to eat.

"Have I worn you out with all my talking?"

"Nope, I could listen to you talk all day."

Truthfully, my feet hurt from all those extra hours I'd been working, and I was just hungry and wanted something to eat. The night before, I hadn't eaten much or slept well because I couldn't wait to see her again. We walked back to the house and Bonnie fixed us both a plate of food. The girl sure could cook. That food was some of the best I had ever tasted. Except, of course, for my mother's, and for Miss Ada's biscuits. When we finished eating I asked Bonnie if I could take a nap.

"Go ahead," she said, and smiled.

She began cleaning the dishes. I took my boots off and lay on her bed. It smelled just like Bonnie and before long I fell asleep. I don't know how long I slept, but when I woke Bonnie was sleeping next to me. She was soft and warm and her hair smelled like jasmine. I knew right then and there that I was going to ask her to be my wife. I started to get up and Bonnie woke as soon as I moved.

"Thanks for everything," I said. "I think it's time for me to be getting on back."
One thing I didn't want was to get caught walking on a road after dark. Nightriders would beat and even kill Negroes caught walking by themselves at night.

"Will I see you tomorrow at church?" asked Bonnie.

"I don't know. I've already missed a lot of my extra days from working and I'm not making as much money as we're gonna need to make our way up North."

"Well, I understand that alright."

As I walked out the door, she walked behind me. When I turned around to say goodbye, Bonnie hugged me. I held her and it felt like my heart was going to jump through my chest. I didn't want to let her go and it seemed like I could have stood there for the rest of my life, just holding her in my arms and breathing in the smell of her jasmine flower scent.

"I hope I see you tomorrow," she whispered softly in my ear.
That warm feeling went through my body and I just about forgot whatever I had said about working.

"We will see," I said, and let her go.

Then I started walking across the yard towards the road. I turned around and saw Bonnie watching me as I walked away. I waved goodbye and started walking on down the road. Those two ladies were still sitting across from Bonnie's house smiling. Once I got back to Woodloe, I went straight to Aunt Fran's House and told her I planned to marry Bonnie.

"Well my goodness boy, you sure did learn a lot about courtin' after just one visit. When's y'all plannin' on gettin' married?"

"I don't know" I said. "I haven't asked Bonnie to marry me yet. I don't even know if she'll have me. I sure hope she will, I hope she feelin' the same way as me."

"Ain't but one way to find out and you know what that is."

"Yeah, I guess I do."

Later that night, I decided I would go to church the next day and ask Bonnie after church was out. So that's what I did. I sat on that hard bench again and listened to that preacher talk for two hours, I even gave him a whole dime for the poor-cent just in case it might bring me some luck with Bonnie. Then finally after the singing and the preaching and the shouting was all over, we walked out the church. I told Bonnie I needed to talk with her and I wanted to walk her home. After she said all of her goodbyes to the Brother Hims and Sister Hers, she was ready to go.

"Um, Miss Bonnie, I, um, know we hadn't known each other all that long or nothin' but I was wonderin' somethin'…"

"You were? What was you wonderin' Isaiah?"

"Well, I feel like you're the right woman for me and, um, I was wondering if maybe you would be my wife."

We had stopped walking, but then she kept on. She

took one step, and then another and another. Finally, she turned around.

"I don't know," she said, "You sure you wants to be married to me?"

"About as sure as I know how to be."

"Then I have to tell you...there were some things...that happened to me back when I was a slave. They wasn't things I wanted to happen, but what I wanted didn't seem important to nobody but me."

Our ages might have been about the same but with her being a female, our experiences as slaves had been different. She said her master and his sons had fancied the pretty and the young slaves. For a moment, she stared at me without saying anything else, then she turned around and pulled her dress down at the shoulders so I could see her back. I saw the scars on her skin from the whippings her masters had given her.

"You sure you want a wife who look like—"

"Bonnie...you don't never have to speak about that no more. That was the past. What I want is for our future."

I knew all too well how slave women and men had been treated on some plantations. I also knew there was nothing they could have done about it without getting killed for doing it.

"I don't love you no less for what you been through. I love you more because you didn't let it stop you from being Bonnie...my Bonnie."

For a good while she just stood there and it sounded for a minute like she might'a been crying or trying not to cry. I wasn't sure what to do or not do. Then she turned around and looked me dead in my eyes.

"What kind of husband walks behind his wife?" she

said. "A husband and wife supposed to walk side by side."

"Does that mean you saying yes?"

"Yes, Mr. Isaiah. That mean I'm sayin' yes."

I let out a loud shout, picked Bonnie up, and hugged her.

"I'll make you the best husband any woman ever had," I shouted.

Then I wiped the tears from her eyes, took her by the hand, and we walked slowly to her house. When we got there, I told her to go ahead, start making plans and choose the day of the wedding. We kissed for the first time. I said goodbye and went back home one happy young man.

At Woodloe, I told Fran she could help plan the wedding with Bonnie and let me know when it was. Aunt Fran started running around like she had gone mad, talking about how much there was to do. I shook my head and told her all we had to do was let that preacher say a few words, watch us jump over a broom, and that would be it. Fran looked at me like I was crazy.

"You let me and Bonnie take care of the wedding part and you just take care of the get married part."

"Well I guess that's alright with me so long as Bonnie becomes my wife, Mrs. Isaiah Jones."

After I left Aunt Fran, I went to Robert's schoolhouse and got him to help me write a nice poem like one of the ones he sometimes read to us. It took some nights after that to get it to his satisfaction, but in the end I thought it was ok and we called it *A Poem for My Bonnie*:

> I walked outside and looked up at the moon,
> I saw no moon, only you.
> The air blew softly on my face,
> Yet I felt only you.

Blood rushed though my body and my heart
Began to ache.
I knew at that moment that for me,
There was only you.
You are my rising sun that slowly breaks
Through the night at dawn,
And the vessel that holds all my dreams at dusk.

I LOVE YOU BONNIE

# ♦ CHAPTER 8 ♦

A few weeks later on Sunday, March 3, the day of the wedding arrived. Bonnie and Aunt Fran had invited everyone from our two plantations to the wedding. Even Lew and his family were there with Robert. I heard that Master Jones wanted to come but wasn't feeling so well and Ada was at the big house taking care of him, but she sent a big cake to let us know we had her blessings.

Some of the white workers were there with their families also. I didn't like that because it made me nervous but I didn't say anything because the fact is just about everybody like an occasion where there's plenty of food and people get to stand around smiling instead of breaking their backs working. I had never seen anything like it in my life. It was like we were putting on some kind of shindig and everyone wanted to be part of it.

I was sure glad I had gone into town a few days before and brought myself a new pair of pants and a new shirt. Fran told me to go to the front of the church and stand there. Seemed to me like I stood there for about an hour before Bonnie came and joined me.

She looked more beautiful than I had ever seen her look before as she walked slowly toward me. She was wearing all white, with white flowers in her hair. And she smelled of jasmine. As she moved close beside me I smiled, took her hand, and turned toward the preacher.

At that moment I felt as if our souls had become one. I didn't hear much of what the preacher was saying except for the part where he asked if I would take Bonnie as my wife.

"I does," I said, but when I heard Robert clear his throat, I corrected myself and said, "I do."

Then he asked Bonnie the same thing.

"Yes, I do," she answered.

After that, we jumped the broom and became husband and wife. Everybody clapped their hands and cheered. The women from the two plantations had cooked all kinds of food. We had a grand time that day. It was probably the best day of my life. Later on I took my wife to my house on Woodloe Plantation to start our lives together. The next day I borrowed one of Master Jones' wagons and took Bonnie to Sheffield Plantation to get her things. We pulled the wagon in front of her house, got out, and began loading it. Bonnie started crying as she put her things into the wagon.

"What's wrong?" I asked.

"I've lived here all my life. I was born in this house and kinfolks say my daddy was born here too. I can't say all my times here have been happy times but..."

I walked over to my new wife and held her close while she cried. Once she was ready, we finished loading the wagon and walked across the yard to say goodbye to the two old women on the porch. They already knew who I was but for the first time I found out they were sisters named May Belle and Stella. One was light brown-skinned and the other dark but both had long black wavy hair that sat in two thick braids over their shoulders. Bonnie had some money coming for the work she had done that year and part of the year before, so we stopped at the big house to see about getting it. She knocked on the back door and a tall dark-skinned lady opened it.

"Hey there Bonnie, this here your new husband?"

"Yes ma'am. We on our way back to Woodloe and I came to see if I can get the money I worked for."

"Well seeing how you worked for it I guess you ought'a be able to get it. Y'all stay here and I'll be back."

When the lady returned, she handed Bonnie sixty whole dollars. This was for six months of hard work in the fields. Bonnie told me she was supposed to be getting ten dollars a month, which came out to what she got. Usually they took out for the things she got from the plantation storehouse, so the most she'd ever gotten before was seventy-three dollars for an entire year. She had been cheated the whole time she worked there and should have been getting paid at least one hundred dollars for the year. They had to have been overcharging her for supplies. With all the cheating they'd been doing, Bonnie had only been able to save eighty-two dollars. There was nothing we could do about it at that point, so I just shook my head and we left.

It seemed to me like white folks could do anything they wanted to do. But I figured that Bonnie got better than some I'd heard about on other plantations. There was talk about folks who never got paid anything at all and couldn't leave plantations because they somehow always ended up owing more money then they was earning. White folks started making them pay something they called rent just for living in the same houses that they had been living in for years. Before we left Sheffield, I told some of the folks on the plantation about how Bonnie had been cheated. I also told them about Robert's schoolhouse and said he could teach them about money so it would be harder for anybody to cheat them.

Since Bonnie was my wife now, whatever me and Fran had, she had. I added her money together with ours and put it all back in the hiding place.

## ◆ CHAPTER 9 ◆

For the rest of that year Bonnie, Fran, and me worked in the fields almost every day. There were three of us now and this meant we would have more money when we got ready to leave. Come the beginning of January the next year, we counted up our money again. We now had two hundred and ninety dollars and thirty-seven cents. Since Andrea had been working in the big house from time to time with Miss Ada, she had managed to save up fifteen dollars.

Things looked good and we were that much closer to our dream coming true. Around the middle of May, I found out that Bonnie was with child. I was going to be a father. This was going to be the first child in the family that wouldn't be born a slave. I was as proud as I could be. Later on I would learn that pride wasn't always a good thing and that it could come back to hurt you. But at the time I didn't think that way.

I was feeling so good one evening that I invited my little cousins over and told the story about Boshama and his many wives and children. After all the story-telling was done and they went back home, Bonnie turned to me and said, "That's the last time you telling that story Mr. Isaiah Jones cause the only wife you gon have is the one you lookin' at right now, and so far as how many children we have is concerned… Well, we'll just have to leave that up to God, won't we?"

"If you and God say so then that's how it's gonna be."

I didn't really understand why she got so upset over something as simple as that story but I figured it didn't matter now that she had spoken what was on her mind. I remembered too Aunt Fran telling me that women who was about to become mamas could get kind'a touchy so I left old Boshama out of any story-telling from that point on.

Things went well enough and Bonnie worked right up until the time came to have our baby. It was now November and we were all in the came fields when I heard my wife scream. Fran and some other women helped to bring a beautiful girl child into this world right there in the cane fields of Woodloe Plantation. Me and some of the women carried Bonnie and our daughter to our house and put them in bed.

I named my daughter Jamie Theodocia Jones. My father's name had been James, and if this child had been a boy I would have named it after him. Theodocia was my mother's middle name. I put Jamie in Bonnie's arms and left them and Fran at our house. I went back to the cane fields where everybody congratulated me and said that I did a good job. I couldn't help thinking that I hadn't done anything. Bonnie was the one who'd done all the work. I stayed in the fields until dusk dark and then headed home to my wife and child. I liked the way that sounded a lot: my wife and child.

As I walked toward the house, I thought about how different my life with my family was going to be from when I had been a child growing up with my mama and daddy. I thought about how different Jamie's would be, growing up without ever knowing anything about being a slave.

When I got near the house, I saw a group of women gathered outside and figured they had all come to take a look at the new baby. Something about the way they stopped talking and looked at me made me walk a little faster. The minute I stepped inside the house, I realized something was very wrong.

"Her bleedin' ain't right," said Aunt Fran.

"What? Bleedin'?"

"Her bleedin's too heavy from the birth and we can't get it to stop. Now listen, if we get it to stop...Isaiah, is you listening?"

"We gotta do somethin' Aunt Fran, we gotta—"

"We is doin' somethin'! Now this what you gotta do for your wife or else we gon lose her."

"What?! Tell me what I gotta do, please, tell me what I gotta do!"

"Go to Miss Lizzy house, tell her your wife just had a baby and she losin' her blood. Now go!"

I started crying as I ran all the way to Miss Lizzy's house. Before I reached her door, she was already standing outside.

"It's about time you got here Isaiah, I been waitin' on you."

"You been waitin'?"

I didn't know how this could be because I hadn't known I was going to her house myself until Aunt Fran sent me. Besides that, she lived in the last house on the edge of the woods and couldn't have heard what was said. Nobody had told her I was coming, but there she was standing and waiting. She put a small brown bottle in my hand and told me to have Bonnie drink the liquid inside. I started to turn and leave when Miss Lizzy said something that I didn't understand.

"Still waters run deep son, and not every life put here meant to be a long life."
Those words tore me up inside and even though I didn't scream the way I felt like doing, so many tears filled my eyes it felt like a burning river was flowing down my face. That was when she did something else strange. She put another little bottle right up under my eyes. I couldn't think or move while she put the bottle under one eye and then the other, my tears just running inside it. I guess the bottle must have filled up because she finally removed it and stuck a cork in the opening. She shook her head and looked at me like she knew things about my life I didn't know myself. A chill ran through me and I trembled.

"I'm gonna hold on to these tears for you Isaiah.

I didn't even ask her why she would want to do something like that, just gave her this strange look and backed away while she turned around and went inside her house. Running back home, I kept thinking about what Miss Lizzy had said and done. Did it mean Bonnie was going to die? That couldn't happen, could it? She was my whole world, my reason for living. The thought of losing her was more than I could bear. I told myself she wasn't going to die, she would be all right.

I ran straight inside the house and gave Fran the little brown bottle. I couldn't stand to see Bonnie so weak and hurt and Fran said there wasn't nothing else for me to do besides pray, so I went to my parents' gravesite. I had already lost the both of them. Wasn't that enough to lose so early in life? I tried to hold back the tears but they kept coming. I cried until I choked, doubled over in pain, and fell on the ground. Looking up at the sky, I asked the Lord to please not let Bonnie die. I asked Him to forgive me for not liking preachers very much and for anything else I might'a done or been that caused Him to get upset with me and make my wife ill.

I don't know if He heard me or not but Bonnie didn't die. Her bleeding stopped. She stayed in bed for three days, sleeping most of the time while Aunt Fran took care of the baby, then she started getting better. My wife was all right and I had a healthy baby girl. I told Bonnie not to worry about going back into the fields for a spell. She was happy to stay home and take care of Jamie and so long as they were both well, I didn't worry too much about how much money we was or wasn't managing to save. Bonnie would sit for hours at a time, holding Jamie and talking or singing to her. When it was time to go to sleep at night, she would put Jamie in the bed between the two of us.

After a while, I took a wood crate and made it into a small bed for our daughter, attaching rounded legs to it so we could rock it. Jamie liked it when we rocked her to sleep. She seemed about as full of love as anybody could be. She would go to anyone who put their hands out to hold her. She was one happy little girl who almost never cried. I guess she never had time to cry with everybody making all the fuss over her the way we all did. Sometimes I had to gently pull her out of Bonnie's hands so the child could sleep in her own bed. Then Bonnie would always rock her to sleep before going to sleep herself. Two or three times a night Bonnie would check on Jamie and we always had candles lit throughout the night to light the room. I figured she was so protective because she had almost died herself and left our little girl without a mother, but later on I would find out it was for another reason.

For the time being, we were all happy and life was good for Bonnie, Jamie, Fran, her kids and me. How could I have known that a time would come when I would miss those days so much?

# ♦ CHAPTER 10 ♦

At the beginning of our fourth year working to save money and make our way North, Fran, Bonnie and I counted up our money to see how we were doing. This time we hadn't done too well. The birth of Jamie and Bonnie's illness afterwards had slowed things down, plus there was a few times when we had no choice but to spend some money on store-bought things for the kids as well as ourselves. We still managed somehow to hold onto four hundred dollars. Little Andrea had eighty dollars of her own money. Altogether, that gave us four hundred and eighty dollars but I didn't want to include Andrea's earnings as part of the going North money cause I felt like that ought'a be set aside for when she was older and might need it for something important. Since she was the one working for it and everything that just seemed proper to me. After one more year, we would leave with whatever we had.

I started to worry about keeping so much money around and got scared someone might try to steal it. With that in mind, I took all our money to Robert's white brother Lew one night and asked him to keep it for us. We wrote down the amount on a piece of paper so we could keep account of it. He took the four hundred and eighty dollars and gave me another sheet of paper that said he had it. That was a load off my mind. I knew I could trust Lew Jones about as much as everybody trusted his school teaching brother and fact is I would have preferred for Robert to keep it but anything could happen to a black man living by himself and doing things his own way like Robert was. Lew was right there in the big house and wasn't nobody likely to go busting in there bothering him and his family. White folks talked about what a hero he was for fighting in the war, and black folks talked about how good he had treated them long before the war.

About a week later, it turned out that I had done the right thing by giving that money to Lew. Bonnie and I came home and saw where someone had been in our house looking through all our stuff. They had turned everything upside down and even found the hiding place underneath the wood-burning stove where we'd kept the money in a clay jar. Before we were free no one would have ever done a thing like that, so I told myself that stealing from your neighbor was a part of being free. Or it may have been some of them poor white folks, the ones as poor as us black folks, that did it. I really didn't know, but I was sure glad I had moved that money before anybody else could get to it. By the springtime, the work had gotten better and we didn't have to work as hard as before. My wife and child were healthy and happy, so were Fran and the kids.

One of Fran's church brothers started chasing after her all the time, bringing her flowers and taking the kids candy from the stores in Savannah. He would be in church every Sunday waiting for Fran. She said she wasn't interested in being courted but the man just didn't know how to take no for an answer. He refused to understand that Fran was never going to get over the loss of her husband.

After all of those years she still hadn't let go of him and the hurt was still very much a part of her. The human heart is a funny thing. A person can be happy and sad at the same time. No one ever talked about Fran holding on to grief the way that she did but at the time none of that seemed to matter because we were all too busy working to make a better future for ourselves.

Then one day we were all in the rice paddies when Andrea came running up to us and crying. She said something was wrong with Jamie. Bonnie and I dropped our tools at the same time and ran as fast as we could to the house with Fran following right behind us.

As we got closer to the house, we saw Will and Brook standing outside screaming. We shot pass them to inside the house and ran to Jamie's bed. It looked to me like my daughter wasn't breathing. I was almost too scared to pick her up, but I did, and that was when I saw it. Curled up under the covers in the corner of her bed was a rattlesnake. I looked at my beautiful little Jamie and saw where the snake had bitten her on the side of her face, and then I gave her to Bonnie. Without thinking about it or hesitating, I grabbed the snake behind its head with one hand and walked slowly over to the table. I picked up the biggest knife had, held the snake down, and chopped its head off. Then I raised the knife again, brought it down hard, and split the head in half.

Bonnie held Jamie and screamed as the baby's tiny body hung limp and lifeless in her arms. The only thing anybody could do was stand next to her and cry, and that's what we did. I kept looking at the snake I had cut to pieces and wondered how it got in the house and crawled into Jamie's bed. Of course, the truth is there was any number of ways it could have done it but I didn't care about the truth. Even though it was already dead, I had a mind to chop it up some more.

Then people started coming in from the fields and the other houses to see what was going on. Most of them started crying when they found out what had happened. Many of them had been right there with us when Bonnie gave birth to Jamie in the middle of a work day right there in the fields and they just couldn't believe our baby was gone so soon. A pain like I never felt before filled my entire body. It grabbed hold of my very soul and shook it until emptiness was the only thing left. At that point, I remembered what Miss Lizzy had said to me, "Still waters run deep son, and not every life put here meant to be a long life."

When she said it, I thought she was talking about Bonnie. Now I knew she was talking about my sweet little baby girl Jamie. As hurt and broken up inside as I was, I told myself I had to move past my own pain and be strong for everyone else, especially Bonnie. After all, I was the head of the family. And they all depended on me. So I made myself stop crying, sat on the floor next to Jamie's bed, and held Bonnie while she rocked back and forth holding Jamie.

For the rest of that day and far into the night, we sat there holding our baby. The sun was about to come up when Fran hugged us both and took Jamie out of Bonnie's arms. This made her cry even louder, but her strength was draining and she couldn't keep it up. Her voice went hoarse and then faded completely. She began to tremble and then she just passed out in my arms. I picked her up and put her in bed. Her body was limp and almost as lifeless as Jamie's had been. She was so weak I could barley understand her when she started saying something about, "Not this one too...please...not this one..."

I didn't understand what she was talking about. The next morning, Bonnie wouldn't move from that bed. She wouldn't eat or drink or talk anything. She soiled herself and still made no attempt to move. She wouldn't look at me when I spoke or touched her. It was as if she had given up on life and just didn't care anymore.

I decided it would be best to bury Jamie that same day. Aunt Fran and some of the other women came to the house, got Bonnie cleaned up and dressed her for the funeral. I made a small wooden box to put Jamie's body in and took it to Fran's house. I had walked across that yard many times but that one time stands out in my mind more than any other. Fran dressed Jamie. Together we put her in the box. Then I closed it.

When I went back home to get Bonnie, she refused to move. She sat on the bed looking at the floor, moaning and slowly moving her head from side to side, as if she was saying, "No."

"I'm sorry," I told her. "I'm sorry Bonnie. Come on."

I picked her up and carried her every step of the way to the graveyard.

Several men had already dug a small grave next to that of my father's and mother's. They had also brought a chair for Bonnie and I sat her on it while I stood beside her holding her hand.

The preacher came to say a few words over Jamie and spoke some more words more softly directly to me and Bonnie, but I don't think either one of us heard exactly what he said. People from both plantations, Woodloe and Sheffield, had come also, which was an amazing thing to see considering they had all been working. I didn't even know how they knew about it because it wasn't something I'd planned on advertising. Surely I had been heartbroken to lose my mother and father, but they at least had been a big part of my life for a good long while. I'd had time to know them and love them, and to make memories of them that I would keep for the rest of my life. There were even times when I had dreams about them so real it seemed like they were still alive. But with Jamie, it seemed like we'd had just enough time to say hello before we were forced to say goodbye.

As I looked at the tiny box that held my daughter, I thought about how proud I'd been the day she was born. All that pride didn't mean so much now. It had all been turned into a burning pain and intense sorrow. I blamed God for this. How could He sit by up in the sky and let this happen to my sweet child? People had always told me God looked after babies and fools. Why hadn't he looked after my baby?

Watching the two men lower Jamie's casket into the ground, Bonnie screamed so loud the sound could have shattered the heart of every angel in heaven. Then she started to shake and fell unconscious against me as if she was dead herself. I carried her home and put her back in our bed.

Bonnie was never the same after that day. The happiness we had found together went out of her and it never returned. After about a month, she still hadn't returned to work. She barely spoke to me or anyone else. She never went back to the Sunday meetings and rarely even left the house. Besides staying with her as much as I could, I didn't know what else to do or say. It was as painful to see her like that as it had been to pick Jamie up out of her bed and see that rattlesnake curled up in the covers. Every day, I just wanted to break down and cry, but I kept on telling myself I had to be strong for her. I was the head of our family and I had to be strong. I also had to find a way to help my wife get better.

Hoping one of Bonnie's old neighbors or friends might be able to help us in some kind of way, I went one day to Sheffield Plantation. The first people I saw were May Belle and Stella, those same two old women who'd been sitting on the porch that first time I visited Bonnie. Talking with them, I learned that sometimes when we go looking for things, sometimes we don't really want to accept what we find out.

The old women had not been to Jamie's funeral, but they had heard about our loss. Before they spoke to me, they looked at each other and slowly nodded, like they were agreeing on something without saying a word. They both wore aprons over their dresses and pulled a pipe out of the pockets. They stared at me and lit their pipes at the same time. They then took turns telling me about something that I'd known was possible but hadn't really thought about where Bonnie was concerned.

"You know Bonnie lost her mama and daddy when she was little, don't chu?" asked Mae Bell.

"Yes'm."

"Even if they'd been alive," added Stella, "wasn't nothin' nobody could'a done to stop the master and his sons from using her the way they did."

"Nothin' at all," said May Belle. "Before freedom come along and before you come along too, lots of us gave birth to babies that was taken away and sold for slaves as soon as they were born."

"Cause that's the way it was," said Stella. "That's what they did with my twins."

"Mine too. Plus my other three sons and two daughters."

"And that's what they did with those two Bonnie had."

"One was a boy and one was a girl. I know 'cause I helped her that first time."

And I helped her that second time."
"She was different from us 'cause bad as it hurt, we learned to accept it and keep on living."

"Cause that's the way it was."

"But your Bonnie couldn't let it go and always talked about how one day she was gon find her babies and have another one all her own so they could stay together and take care of each other."

"She gave up on that idea 'bout findin' the ones they took from her when you asked her to be your wife."

"She figured God meant for you and her to make a free family together, so she put all that pain over the children that was taken away behind her."

"Now this terrible thing come and happen with your new baby, the one she thought was gonna make up for the past, and she about as lost as a lost soul can be."

"That's a hard kind'a hurt to fix Mr. Isaiah. You gotta give her as much love as you can plus even more than that and pray as hard as you can too."

"She said y'all was gon leave and make a better life up North, so this might be a good time to do it Mr. Isaiah."

"Yessuh, this just might be that time."

My head throbbed and ached as I struggled to understand everything they had just told me. Before Jamie, Bonnie had had another daughter and son who'd been sold off as slaves before she had a chance to hold them or anything else. She'd never seen either of them again after they were born. Besides her just loving the child we'd had together, this was another part of the reason Bonnie was taking Jamie's death so hard.

Back home, I told her I'd been to see Stella and Mae Belle and said we'd had a long talk about the things that happened before we got married. It wasn't no way for a man to fully understand something like that and the most I could do was tell her my love would never change and I would always be there for her. I told her that if she wanted to we could have other children once we got off Woodloe.

"I'll do whatever it is you want Bonnie. But you gotta come back to me so I can help you. So we can help each other. Ok? Whatever it takes to bring you back your happiness, I'm gonna do it."

Even though I must'a said about a hundred things that night, fact is I didn't know what to do. The thought of going back to Miss Lizzy for help didn't make me feel so good but I went anyway. She wasn't standing outside but her door was open and she sat in a chair in the dark. This time, though, she didn't have any small bottles to give me. When she spoke, it was like the night itself was talking.

"Son your wife got a hard fight on her hands right now and can't nobody fight it for her but her. Some years back, that teacher-man Robert had to fight for his body and soul after Isaac beat him down so close to death that didn't nobody think he'd stay in this world, and if it hadn't been for his white brother Lew and Old Jordan, he probably would'a left it."

"Well Bonnie got me to live for, don't she? Don't she got me?"

"Now that's a sho' 'nuff fact, she do. But son, for a woman that gives birth, there is no stronger bond than the one between her and that child, from the time it enter her belly 'til the time they both ain't nothin' but a memory. It ain't so much that she lost this baby that's got her fightin' for her life. It's that so much  life been taken from her, the life that come through her body and the life of her own self."

It would be some years before I really understood what Miss Lizzy said that night but eventually I would. Listening to her, it felt like my heart was gonna swell and pop right out'a my chest. But it didn't. It just hurt. I remembered that somewhere in that cabin, Miss Lizzy already had my tears in a little brown bottle, so I told myself it wasn't no use crying anymore. I needed to get back home and see about Bonnie.

Two months after we had buried Jamie, I was sound asleep one night after a long day and a long week of working to make up for lost time. I had been trying to work twice as hard because Bonnie was still unable to work and I figured the sooner we were able to leave, then the sooner might get better.

So I had come home and gone to bed on that particular night without even eating supper. I knew Fran or Andrea had made sure Bonnie ate and I didn't have to worry about that. Until I woke up the next morning, I had no idea that Bonnie had left the house. At first, I was surprised just because she had gone out, period, and then I was kind of glad because her going out was a good sign that she might be getting better. I figured she must have gone to Fran's house and went to join her over there. When Fran and the children said none of them had seen her, my heart sank and I knew something was very wrong.

We looked all over the plantation for her, going from cabin to cabin and searching through the fields with no luck at all. I went next to Sheffield plantation but no one there had seen her either.

That afternoon, Miss Lizzy told us she had seen someone the night before walking on the east end of the plantation. She hadn't been able to make out exactly who it was, she said, but knew it was a woman and knew she was troubled. I had a feeling she knew a lot more than she was telling but just didn't want to be the one to say it. The east end of the plantation was filled mostly with rice paddies leading toward swamp land. A place like that was dangerous enough during the daytime and downright deadly at night.

We found Bonnie's body going towards evening, just before it got too dark to search anymore. My beautiful wife had walked straight into the swamp and to her death. For the last time, I carried her back home and put her on our bed.

As I had done so many times before, I went to my parents' burial ground. Sitting on the ground next to my father's and Jamie's grave, I felt like I was no longer alive myself. Everything in me wanted to cry but the tears wouldn't come. I must have sat there for a very long time because Aunt Fran came looking for me. With all she had been through herself, and all she had seen me go through, she could barely talk, and for a while she didn't even try. When she did, she had to squeeze the words out past the pain.

"No matter what's going through your head right now Isaiah Jones—"

"I should'a stayed awake last night and took care of her , and made sure—"

"You hush up now, wasn't nothing you coulda'—"

"I should'a asked her if she needed somethin'—"

"Don't you be talkin' no nonsense like that. You did everything—"

"I should'a came home early and—"

"You did everything it was in your power to do! Couldn't nobody ask for more than that. Don't you go thinkin' bad about yourself, you hear me? You did everything you could do."

I didn't know if Bonnie had done what she did because of a broken heart or the fact that she just didn't want to live anymore. All I knew for sure was that I had lost the two things in this world that I loved the most. I also knew that as long as I lived I would never love anybody the way I loved Bonnie and Jamie, my wife and daughter. You might say somewhere deep in my soul a hole opened that would never mend or close. It was something I would learn to live with every day of my life. I began to understand that Miss Lizzy had been talking about Bonnie when she said, "still waters ran deep," but then about Jamie when she added, "not all life is meant to be long."

I never got rid of my wife's and my daughter's belongings. Each day when I came from working in the fields I saw them and I thought about the two women I loved. Sometimes I could smell Bonnie's scent of jasmine when a soft breeze blew and I felt like she was somewhere near me. I wanted to think she was in Heaven with our little Jamie, holding her and keeping her safe. I would never love another woman the way I loved Bonnie. I would miss her every day of my life. Still, after her passing, I had to be strong: Fran and the children were still alive and they were all depending on me.

# ♦ CHAPTER 11 ♦

The days after Bonnie's death went by slowly. Most of the time, week after week, and month after month, I worked without even knowing what day it was. Then that special day finally came when it was time for us to leave Woodloe Plantation.

We decided we would go to Washington D.C. because Robert said that was where the president of the country lived, so we figured if it was good enough for the president then it would be good enough for us too. Truth is, Robert gave me all kinds of advice during that last week before we took off. We met at his schoolhouse late at night and one of the first things he told me was to put my money in a bank as soon as I got settled. I didn't ask how he knew about the money because everybody knew him and his brother Lew had been close all their life and getting Lew to keep it for me had been pretty much the same as getting Robert to keep it.

"Always dress clean when you go to a bank," he said, "That way the people you're dealing with will treat you like a respectable business man and help you get whatever need. If you go in there dressed like a field slave, they'll treat you like one. After you get yourself a house, make sure you keep up your schooling and make sure your little cousins keep theirs up too."

To hear Robert talk, you would'a thought he was the granddaddy of the world but he actually was just a few years older than I was at the time, which means if I was about nineteen soon to be twenty, then he was about twenty-six soon to be a hundred. I never had to ask how he got to be so old at such a young age because one time I didn't find him at the school so went looking around his cottage next to it and found him out back without a shirt on. Everywhere you looked on his body there was a scar left over from that awful beating he'd gotten from Isaac and that people said had almost killed him. Looking at those scars, you had to wonder how it was he didn't die. Even though I had never been beaten the way he had, I believed I knew what that pain was like. He didn't say anything when he saw me staring, just smiled and put his shirt on.

Mister Jones sold me a wagon for five dollars. I had to do a little work on it but it was good as new when I was finished with it. Then I got a mule from the Union soldiers in Savannah for seven dollars. Fran and the children loaded all their things in the wagon and told all their friends goodbye.

That night before we left, I went to visit the graves of my loved ones. Sitting down on the ground, I talked with my mother and father, and with Bonnie and Jamie. I told them we were leaving and promised to look after the family. I said I would never forget them and everything they had taught me. Grabbing a hand full of dirt, I put it in my pocket and said goodbye.

Woodloe was someplace I would always love. Just like Miss Lizzy had said; it would always be a part of me and I would always be a part of it. But the only things I took with me when we left were some bittersweet memories and my clothes. Things belonging to my mother, my father, Bonnie, and Jamie were left at Woodloe Plantation. Why? Because they were more a part of Woodloe than the place where we were going. Woodloe was where they had lived and died, and where they had been most happy or sad. So that's where their things belonged and that's all I have to say about it

When the morning came and it was time for us to leave, we all got in the wagon and headed down the dirt road the led off the plantation. I made one last stop at the graveyard. Fran and the kids stayed in the wagon as I walked over to where the people I loved were buried and promised once again that I would remain humble and be strong for Fran and the kids. Then I got back in the wagon, started driving north, and never looked back once.

# ♦ CHAPTER 12 ♦

Robert had said it would be best to travel with the Union solders when heading north. There were still a lot of former slave holders who hated Negro people and weren't none too happy about losing the war even thought talk had it they were the ones who started it in the first place.

Most of the money we had saved was sewn into Fran's undergarments. I kept twenty-five dollars with me as we traveled. As far as anyone would know, we didn't have much of anything. That was exactly how I wanted it. However, truth be told, between the food Fran had cooked and sold to other workers, working my own double shifts every chance I got, and what Bonnie had made, we had saved eight hundred and forty-three dollars and fifty cents. Andrea had saved one hundred and eighty-three dollars of her own.

It was about eight o'clock in the morning when we headed for the Union soldiers' camp, right outside Savannah just before you crossed the bridge to go into South Carolina. As we headed for the camp, we rode down a lot of long dusty roads. On one of them, I saw something strange. It looked like someone had put a scarecrow in a tree. But I knew right away this wasn't no scarecrow.

"Oh my lawd sweet Jesus," said Fran.

"Mama what's that?" the kids asked.

"Don't let them look Fran, cover their eyes!"

As we got closer to the tree where the dead body hung, a chill ran though my bones and I became truly afraid. But I stayed quiet because I had promised to be strong. As we passed the hanging body, I looked up and recognized it as Joe, the man who had owned the juke joint back in the woods. I recalled how impressed I had been to see him dressed as fine as any white man that first time I went to Savannah. Now here he was, hanging from a tree just as plain as day, fancy clothes and all. Looked to me like he had been there for some time and the smell was awful.

I wondered who did this and why. In the back of my mind I already knew the answers. Joe had become what some people called "uppity," and most white folks hated uppity Negroes. They all knew Joe had money by the way he dressed, walked, and talked, and they sure didn't like it. But then a lot of blacks hadn't liked it either. I recalled the men on Woodloe talking about how Whites had started running Joe's juke joint. No one had seen him around for a long time. Now I knew why.

I hurried the mule on pass Joe and down that road. Still the stench had filled the air and seemed to have gotten into the wagon. It was like Joe's soul was trying too late to catch a ride with us. That smell followed us for more than a mile before it finally faded away.

While riding along, I thought about how good it was going to be not to live in fear anymore. One reason I had

spent almost all of my time on Woodloe even after the
freedom came was because I had felt safe there. Now we
were heading about as far away from the plantation as we
could get and I prayed we could get there without
something happening to us. Once we got to the Union
soldiers' camp, I signed us in and told a sergeant we were
headed to Washington D.C.

"Can you tell me how long it take to get there?" I
asked.

"Generally speaking, with stops along the way and
picking up travelers like you and your family, and
presuming the weather treats us kindly, it'll be around
twenty-one to twenty-five days."

Since it was early March, the weather should be in
our favor. I had chosen to leave that time of year for that
very reason. Aside from me, Fran, and the kids, I counted
five other Negro families, about twenty single people, and
to my surprise four white families heading north also. Why,
I wondered, would white folks be leaving the South and
moving to the North. It had always seemed to me like they
had everything. The whole South belonged to them. Then it
hit me that they were just like the white workers back on
Woodloe, which meant they were just like me, trying to get
someplace where they could live a better life.

In fact, there were a whole lot of poor white folks
worse off than we were. I saw them every day as we went
from town to town and state to state, from Georgia to South
Carolina, to North Carolina, and right on up the road. If we
hadn't been with Union soldiers, they would have robbed
us and taken everything we had, then most likely would
have killed every last one of us. You could see the hate in
their eyes when they looked at you. You could see a lot of

different things in their eyes when they looked at you. Sometimes it was fear or desperation, and then other times it was hatred that filled the air and prowled around you like a rabid dog.

Thank the Lord we didn't try to make that trip by ourselves. From time to time, we came across more dead Negroes who had been left hanging from trees or on the side of road. Once we saw what looked like a whole family, a father, mother and two little children, all of them hanging from trees and their bodies burnt. What could those folks possibly have done to anyone to deserve something like that? I couldn't help thinking that they could have been us. I felt sorry for them as the soldiers stopped just long enough to cut them down and bury them. I thought about how the folks they left back on their plantation might be wondering how they were doing, and never know that they all had been killed. I never got over seeing that. Will asked me why white folks hated us and why they did these things to us. I didn't have an answer for him then and I still don't. I just don't know. I guess some of them are just full of hate.

We moved along day after day, mile after mile, taking on more folks as we went. Then we came to something called the Mason Dixon line. One of the soldiers said it separated the North from the South. I never did see any line and from where I stood the North and the South both looked the same. But it must have been there all the same because two days later we were in Washington D.C.

# ♦ CHAPTER 13 ♦

Washington D.C. turned out to be a grand place with its beautiful monuments and parks, a whole lot more than anything I had dreamed about or seen until that point. And there were lots of Negro folks walking around in nice clothes. The streets were clean and many of the white folks spoke to you. In the South, most white men outside of Woodloe Plantation would rather have spit on a black man than say, "Good morning." All that foolishness seemed to be behind us now. We had to find somewhere to live and we didn't have to be afraid anymore. After all our years of working hard and saving up money, it felt real good to be in the same city where the president lived.

Robert had told me and Fran to act real casual-like after we got to D.C. so people wouldn't try to take advantage of us being new to the place. After we arrived, we did just that, walked around looking casual-like. Since it wouldn't do for us to sleep in that wagon now that we were off the road, we had to find a place to stay for the night. I spoke with a couple of clean-dressed black men who told me the southeast side of town was a nice part to live in.

Folks that lived in Washington D.C. just called it D.C. and I started doing the same right away.

We got back in the wagon and headed for the southeast part of D.C. where we found a boarding house and got two rooms. After we unloaded the wagon, I put the mule in a nearby stable. We put most of Fran's things in my room since I was the only one in it. The next day I began looking for a place to live and a job.

Fran got dressed up and put our money in a bank. They gave her something called a bank book that told her how much we had in the bank. Just like what Lew gave me when I gave him the money to keep for us. Except for at this bank, the people said the longer they kept the money the more money we would have. They called this interest. It didn't sound right to me, but I figured maybe they do things a bit different in the North.

I got some work with my wagon, hauling furniture and trash and other things for folks. This took me all over Washington and into parts of Maryland and Virginia too. I found out quickly, exactly like Robert had said that you can't trust everybody. When I agreed to help one man move some of his things across town, he said he would pay me seventy-five cents. Once I finished the job, he said he only had twenty-five cents and would pay me the rest of the money later. I never saw that man again, but I learned my lesson that day and began to get the money before I moved things for people.

Soon after that I heard about a government program where people could learn a trade and get a job working for the government. This sounded good to me, and then I found out that by working for the government, you could get help buying a new brand house. Fran and I needed to get out of the boarding house as soon as we could and a job with the government seemed just the way to do it.

I managed to get one of them government jobs and learned to work as a janitor. Back in Savannah they would have called it working as a "house slave" before freedom came. The work paid fifteen cents an hour and I worked nine to ten hours every day. This meant I could make a dollar and thirty-five or a dollar and fifty cents a day, which usually gave me about seven dollars a week, though working for the government we mostly got paid every two weeks or once a month. That was good money for a black man back in those days. We sure didn't get that kind of money hiring out in the South. Besides, the work was mostly all inside work, which meant that I worked every day, rain or shine, Monday to Friday. I didn't have to fret none about the heat or the cold. It sure beat working in the fields in Savannah.

What Fran found was work as a maid for a Negro U.S. senator named Hiram Revels and his wife, which meant that in a way she was working for the government like me. However, they only paid her ten cents an hour for ten-hour shifts. This came to a dollar a day or six dollars a week since she usually worked from the beginning of the week Monday straight on through to Saturday. So that was good money too. Together we could make almost seven hundred dollars a year. We might have even more depending on how many extra days I might work or whatever kind of side jobs I could get.

One day in July, Fran and I went to buy a house. We walked in the realty office and asked to speak to someone about buying a house. I don't know if it was the clothes we had on or what. For some reason the people there looked at us like we were trash. We sat for nearly an hour before anyone even spoke to us. In the office, I smelled jasmine and thought about Bonnie. I could see her sitting on a bench smiling, with the sunlight shining on her skin as she shelled a basket of green beans, and thought how she should have been there with us. Then I tried not to think like that anymore.

When we did finally speak with someone, the first thing he said was we would need three hundred dollars up front to get the house. He said he understood if we didn't have it, and we could come back in a few years when we did. You should have seen his face when we told him that we had it. He turned as red as a beet in the face. Then he called someone else to start the paper work.

The next day, Fran and I went back to the realty office with the money. A manager informed us that since I hadn't been working with the government for a year yet, we would need a hundred dollars more. They said it was for something called a security-deposit. I told the man that we had it and I would be back later that day. That's when the folks in the office started saying "Yes Sir" and "Yes Ma'am" to Fran and me, which was the first time any white folks had ever called us that. We filled out all the papers that afternoon and about a week later we got our house.

Boy was that house a pretty sight. It wasn't no mansion like Mister Jones' big fancy place on Woodloe but it was a whole lot more than the old slave cabin that I had grown up in and called my "house." It had three bedrooms, a kitchen, and a big front room, an inside bathtub with two hand pumps in the house to run water and a big room under it all that was called a basement. It was built out of bricks and not wood like most of the ones I'd seen down south.

That let me know it would be there for a long time.

I told Fran that we could turn the basement into the boys' bedroom. Will and Brook liked that idea because the basement was made part way in the ground with windows on two sides of it and a door that led to the back yard. This allowed them to watch folks as they walked pass our house without being seen and they could come and go without anybody knowing it.

We moved right on in it, and Fran put the kids in a good school that was near to where we lived. In fact you could see the school from our back yard. Fran and the kids seemed happy because our dream had now come true. I started going at night to the same school as the kids after I got off my job. They had classes for us grown folks that wanted to further our education.

Robert had got me started reading and writing to the point that I had developed a love for learning. I really enjoyed taking those classes and learned a lot more about the world than I ever imagined there was to learn. It was lot a bigger too than I'd ever thought, much bigger than just the South or the North, and even bigger than just America and the land of Africa where my people's people had come from.

Yes life was good, we owned our own house and we didn't have to live in fear anymore. The new house cost us fifteen dollars a month, which left us with thirty-seven dollars of our paychecks to do everything else with. The only thing I didn't like was not really knowing the folks who lived around us, and that small yard in the back of the house. I needed a place to put my mule and wagon but the back yard was much too small for them. After a while I sold them to a man from Maryland for more than I had paid

Mister Jones for them. I wished I could have kept them but just didn't have the room.

# ♦ CHAPTER 14 ♦

Things went well for our family until that first winter in D.C. None of us had ever seen much snow at all until we woke up one cold December morning and looked outside. We saw snow in big white heaps everywhere we looked. It was like somebody put loads of white powder on everything. I got dressed and headed out the door to work. Let me tell you, I didn't make it too far before I started slipping and sliding and falling all over the place. I couldn't stand steady and every time I tried to walk, I fell. I couldn't take two steps without falling.

I ended up crawling back into the house, wet from head to toe and about half frozen. The kids and Fran stood in the front room laughing at me. They were on the floor holding their bellies in pain from laughing so hard. I had to laugh at myself. I guess I did look rather silly doing the "falling man dance." That's the name that Brook gave it. I come to find out later that I had to shovel the snow from the steps and walkway in front of the house then put some rock salt on them to keep it off.

Until that first snowfall, I don't believe any of us

had thought too much about how different the weather would be up north. What we called cold in the South was more like warm compared to the cold we felt up in D.C. Snow had been something that fell in little bits and pieces every other year or so and usually disappeared by the time it hit the ground. Now it gave us a good reason to spend some of our savings on heavy coats, boots, long underwear, and gloves to adapt to the new climate. Despite the fact these were things we needed to survive, we didn't just buy the clothes and start wearing them right away. We wrapped them up as presents and piled them around a Christmas tree so our first Christmas in D.C. was a real special one. I had never seen Fran so happy as when she watched her children open up those pretty fancy boxes and pull out brand new clothes that had been store-bought just for them. That was like something more than a dream, to see them so joyful and free.

The kids loved the snow. They and the other children in the neighborhood would play in it for hours at a time until we made them little fools come in the house. By that time, every one of them would have a runny nose. Yes, we all fell in love with Washington D.C., our new life and our new home.

Still, every once in a while I would think about Woodloe Plantation and my folks, Bonnie, and Jamie. Whenever this happened, I would remind myself of the things we all had lived though and then go on with my life. I kept telling myself that it wasn't how I had lived in the past that mattered the most but how I was living in the present and how I would live in the future.

The years passed and the children grew bigger and smarter.

I saw each one of them change right before my very eyes
from three little shy quiet children from the South into
outspoken and outgoing youth. They were always doing
this, that, or the other thing. Made me tired half the time
just to watch them. I think that children need to sit still
sometimes. You can move so much sometimes that you
out-move your own thinking.

Once we were just plain old Georgia Geeches with
time to sit, talk, tell stories and think. Now we had become
city folk, running around and always in a hurry. That ain't
no kind of way to live. I told Fran to slow them children
down, but she didn't listen. Washington had changed us all.
There had been a time when Fran would have listened to
my every word, especially since she was the one who'd
said I was the man of the family. Now she acted like she
just didn't care what them children did, as long as they
were happy and she got to dress up in fancy uniform
dresses for her job with the senator.

With a nice house, a good job, and lots of new
church friends, it became easy to forget what was important
in our lives. Sometimes we get to busy for our own good,
and that might be what happened to us. When we lived on
Woodloe, we might'a worked some long hard days but we
generally made time for each other. Aside from working
together side by side right there in the fields, we would
have dinner together when it suited us and go fishing
together. Sometimes we would meet with the other folks on
the plantation and have a big eating outside in a big
wildflower field. No, life on the plantation hadn't been all
bad. We had a lot of good days enjoying our lives and life
at a much slower pace.

# ♦ CHAPTER 15 ♦

Seven long years had passed since Mister Jones told us we were all free like him. We'd had two years in D.C. to almost forget where we came from and what all we had been through. I still bore the deep cutting sorrow of my wife and daughter. Unlike my little cousins, I would never be able to forget our past completely.

Will was now twelve years old. Although he'd always been a curious and adventurous boy, he had never been a reckless or dangerous one until we got to D.C. Back on the plantation, he'd always been eager to talk about whatever he had learned in Robert's school. Now he started missing school and hanging around on the streets and in the alleys with a group of boys his age and older. He came in the house all hours of the night. When I asked him about it, he said he was with his friends. Seeing them walking around together, talking loud and cussing and acting tough with each other, I knew sooner or later there would be some serious trouble.

Word came to me that Will had started doing something called running numbers for the Bolito man. That meant he would go around the neighborhood collecting numbers that people bet on along with their hard-earned money. He would write how much they gave him along with the numbers they were betting on in a little notebook. Then he would turn them in to the man he worked for. Until he was done collecting and turned everything in, he had money on him all the time. It wasn't long before everybody in the neighborhood knew it. One night I waited up for him to come in so we could talk.

"Will do you know it's way past midnight?"

"Huh?! It is?"

"Yeah it is and we done had this conversation before so don't stand there and play stupid. You don't see me coming in this house past midnight and you don't see your mama doing it and both of us grown enough to do it, so what make you think a boy twelve years old ought'a being doin' it?"

"My friends—"

"What your friends do ain't my business but what you do is, and what I'm hearing is you running numbers for that bolito man."

"I ain't runnin' no bolito. And even if I was, you ain't my daddy. My daddy dead just like yours."

The minute the back of my hand knocked him on his behind I knew I shouldn't have done it. I didn't believe in hitting human beings because I'd seen too many with their spirits broken by the lash. But that boy had picked the wrong words to be sassy. On top of that, we both knew he was lying.

"You right. I'm not your father. And I've never tried to be your father, but I am your family and I swore on your daddy's grave and my daddy's grave too that I would do my best to look after you and everybody else in our family."

After that, he hung around the house for a day or two and acted the way people expect a twelve year old boy to act. Then he started doing the same things all over again. I told Fran what Will had been doing even though I had a feeling she already knew. Why she never said a word about it was something I couldn't figure out. I did notice though that she started working a lot of shifts that required her to work overnight to "be on call." That meant she didn't have to do no real jobs unless something came up.

"They pay extra when I work the on call shift," she said.

"Yeah I know Aunt Fran but right now I think your son needs you here in this house at night more than that senator or his family needs you in theirs. And besides that, with the money we got saved and the money we making, we can let go of the extra for a while."

"You can let go of your extra if you wanna," she said, "but I ain't lettin' go of mine."

After that, I was done talking. As bad as Will's behavior bothered me, in some ways Fran's bothered me even more. And then too, it worried me to think how all this might be effecting the other children, Andrea and Brook.

Then one Friday night a couple of weeks later, Will didn't come home at all. He had never done anything like that before and I figured he must'a stayed at one of his "friend's" house without saying anything. I waited all day on past evening time before going out to look for him. When I found the group of boys he hung with, all of them claimed they didn't know where he was. I believed they did but I couldn't prove it. I walked around all that night and most of the next day, going into neighborhoods I'd never been in before, but I didn't find him.

Around ten o'clock the next morning, a Sunday morning, I went back home only to find out that he still wasn't there. By then, Fran said she was going out to look for him. I convinced her to stay home with Andrea and Brook and said I would go back out and look some more after I got a few hours sleep.

As soon as my eyes closed good, I started dreaming that I was standing on a river bank waiting for something and all of a sudden Bonnie came walking across the water. She stopped right there in the middle of the river, stood on top of the water with waves sparkling light all around her, and said, "The most you can do for another person is everything you can. After that, it's up to them, no matter how young or how old they may be. Thank you for giving me everything you could."

Just as I was about to dive in the river and swim to her, somebody knocked real heard on the front door and I woke up. The next thing I heard was Fran screaming, "No! Not my child! Oh no God not my Will!"

I jumped from the bed and headed for the front living room.

"What's going on here? Where Will at?"
One of Will's friends stood in the doorway with two more standing behind him. I asked again what was going on.

"Uh, Mr. Isaiah, we found Will down there by the railroad yard so we went and got police cause he ain't alive no mo'. He dead. The police took his body to the morgue and they said somebody kin to him gotta come look at it."

Just before Fran could hit the floor, I caught her and

carried her to her bed. Leaving Andrea sitting beside her and Brook standing by the bed, I went to the morgue and identified Will's body. However much money he'd had was gone along with the bolito book. Someone had robbed and killed him for whatever he'd had in his pockets at the time.

Damn fool boy, why hadn't he listened? I thought about how in the South all we'd had to worry about so far as killing went was the white folks. Now in the North, we had to worry about our own folks too. I knew Negroes had killed Will because Whites didn't come to the part of town where he'd been found. Most stayed around the northwest area or outside of DC.

Suddenly it was like the world had gone mad with Negroes killing Negroes. Only it hadn't mattered all that much to me until I saw Will in that morgue. I never thought I would live to see a day when that happened but there he was. I was as mad at him for getting himself killed as I was heartbroken to see him dead. Truth is, I was too mad to cry and that scared me pretty bad. I had thought our family was done with that kind of pain. I was wrong.

# ♦ CHAPTER 16 ♦

After Will's death, Fran wouldn't let Andrea and Brook go anywhere without her. Not even to the schoolhouse unless she walked with them. She stopped going to work and at first the senator and his wife was all understanding and everything but eventually she lost her job.

Then Fran started doing something I had never seen her do before: drinking gin alcohol. At first she said she drank it to calm her nerves. Next, so she could sleep. Finally, so she could try to deal with the loss of her son, Will.

We always said how much he looked every bit like his father Calvin right down to his smile, and Will's death brought back painful memories of him. Fran's alcohol drinking got to the point where she wouldn't eat half the time. She stopped taking care of herself and even stopped going to church. She didn't want to see her friends, or do much of anything. Andrea and Brook tried to talk to her, but she didn't seem to care about anything they had to say. So we all stood by feeling helpless and watched Aunt Fran slowly drink herself into an early grave.

What could we do? We tried everything we knew. Talking, crying, pleading, begging and praying. If we hid her bottles, she would sneak out and buy another one. We told people not to sell it to her. She would find a bootlegger in a different neighborhood and get it from him. We took her money and she would still get her gin. Then strange people would come to the door saying that she owed them money.

I watched as my aunt Fran went from a strong healthy woman to just a shadow of the woman she once was, the woman who had told me when it was time to be a man and who had worked just as long and hard in the fields of Woodloe Plantation as me. The worse their mother got, the more Andrea and Brook curled up somewhere and cried. They kept asking me to do something, but I didn't know what else I could do. After all, Fran was the eldest of us, she was my mother's younger sister, something she had reminded me of over and over again.

Since we got our freedom, I had seen this drinking sickness many times. I first saw it at Joe's juke joint. Now Fran reminded me of that lady, Miss Lilith, who had asked me to buy her a drink and called me "no-count" because I didn't have any money. Fran had the same look in her eyes that lady had, and her skin was dry and ashy. You could smell the alcohol coming out of her skin. Then after thinking about it for a while, I decided that if we couldn't stop Fran from drinking, we could try to at least keep her in the house. I would get her the gin, and keep it there, so she wouldn't be drunk out in the streets. This didn't work either. I learned that people who have the drinking sickness don't like to drink alone. They crave the company of other people with the same sickness.

It wasn't long before Fran was leaving the house and staying out all day and night. She seemed to not care that she had a house and children to come home to. She didn't seem to care about anything. I spent a lot of time walking the streets looking for her. It's a bad thing to see someone you love laying in the street with no idea of where she is or even who she is. It is bad when you see a man in that kind of shape but it's even worse when the person is a woman. My heart would hurt every time I had to find her and bring her home.

I couldn't stop thinking about all the hell she had survived just to end up like this. Wasn't no telling what all people had done to her during her lifetime. Still she didn't seem to care that she still had two beautiful children who needed their mother, or that we had come as long and far as we had. She put us through pure living hell for the next two years. Worrying about their mother all the time, the children did badly in school and I had to stop going to night classes myself. Andrea and Brook's classmates teased them about their mother's public drunkenness. Brook, who was nine years old when his brother Will died, started having night scares and would wake up screaming and crying.

Then one cold day in November, when Fran had not come home the night before, I went out to look for her and I found her sleeping on the cold ground behind a store. Her coat was gone and she was balled up and trembling as she lay there. I picked her up and took her home like I had done so many times before. Andrea washed her mother off and put her to bed.

Later that night, Fran woke up coughing violently. It got so loud and hard that Fran started coughing up blood.

We got a doctor as soon as we could. He spent some time alone with Fran then called me to the side and said there was nothing he could do to make her better. He gave her a shot that put her to sleep and prescribed some pills for her pain. Then he said she only had a day or two to live.

I don't know about anybody else, but if I only had a few days to live, I'd at least try to do something meaningful with the time I had left. I guess Fran knew it was too late or maybe she just wanted to die. Pain pills or no pain pills, she just wanted to drink alcohol.

Then a few days later, like the doctor had said she would, Fran passed away. I buried her alongside her son Will. It rained so much that day I thought the angels were crying for Aunt Fran. As sad as I was, I didn't cry myself while I held on to Andrea and Brook to help ease their pain. I hadn't cried for Will either. For a minute I wondered why, then I recalled Miss Lizzy holding that little jar under my eyes and collecting my tears. Maybe that was all I'd had left.

Aunt Fran didn't have to die so young. She was a good woman. I know she blamed herself for Will's death. I blamed myself for both of them dying. Maybe things would have turned out differently if we'd just left Woodloe and got one of those houses like other Negroes near Savannah. Folks say mothers don't have favorites when it comes to their children but that's not always true. I always knew Will was Fran's favorite child, and so did Andrea and Brook. I guess that really don't matter now. Does it?

# ◆ CHAPTER 17 ◆

Fran's funeral convinced me that I couldn't risk losing any more of my family. I told myself I would do whatever I had to do to protect Andrea and Brook. I was determined to keep them safe from other people and from themselves if need be.

Once again the words of Miss Lizzy kept coming back to mind: "Every life wasn't put here to be a long life." Was Miss Lizzy talking about my whole family? Was my life going to be cut short also? I wondered what would happen to Andrea and Brook if I suddenly passed away. I told myself that wasn't going to happen and stopped thinking about it.

Springtime came to Washington and the city was beautiful with its cherry-blossom trees but the children were grieving the loss of their brother and mother, so they didn't really notice. Young children never really get over their mother dying. I never got over mine, so I knew the pain they were feeling.

As time went on, the children somehow began to excel in their studies. Andrea was about to finish high school and start nursing school. Brook still had a few years to go. The suffering they had gone through seemed to make them very serious-minded and motivated them to live the lives their brother and mother had lost. I went to work every day and took night classes twice a week.

Andrea finished high school, went on to nursing school, and after two years became a real-life nurse. She looked so nice in her uniform with the white dress, the white stocking things and white shoes. She even wore a small white cap on her head. I never told her how proud I was of her because I remembered what pride had done for me at Woodloe Plantation. But the fact is, I was very proud of her and wished Fran had been there to see what her daughter had become, something neither one of us would have dreamed was possible during our Woodloe days.

She found work at a hospital not far from where we lived. The people she worked with liked her and she made good money, more money than me in fact, even though I'd been on my job for quite some time now. That was alright with me because she had managed to overcome some terrible losses in her young life and studied hard to earn the money she was making. I felt maybe our lives had finally started to get better, and I prayed all the bad times were behind us.

Not long after Andrea became a young working woman, she met a young man named Lenny Penrose. It was bound to happen sooner or later, her meeting boys and such. Andrea had always been a very good-looking girl, just like her mother had been, and boys had always tried to talk her into letting them keep her company. She'd never had time for them and always put her studies first. Although I knew some fast talking buck would try to sweet talk her sooner or later, I didn't like this Lenny guy. My gut told me something about him wasn't right. Like the old folks on the plantation would say, "My soul didn't agree with him."

Andrea spent a lot of her free time with him. They would go out to eat or go for long walks and he would even bring her pretty flowers to the house. One evening as they were sitting in the living room, I asked Lenny what he did for a living.

"I'm a porter Mr. Isaiah."

"How you mean, like workin' in one of those fancy hotels?"

"No sir, I'm a porter for the railroad."

"Oh I see, what some people call land sailors, on account of how you fellas go from city to city and don't stay in one place too long."

He smiled when I said that and I looked at Andrea to catch her reaction. She didn't seem to think it was important.

"I do travel up and down the East Coast but D.C. is what you might call my main port. In fact I've been to Savannah a few times, where Andrea tell me y'all came from straight off the plantation."

I had to admit it was extraordinary to think of him working on a train traveling back and forth between the North and the South, almost like he was doing it for fun, whereas we had come to D.C. in a wagon pulled by a mule, and just like he said, "straight off the plantation." But he still didn't impress me any at all. I thought to myself that he probably had a woman in every city he went to. As soon as he left, I told Andrea that she would do a lot better if she found someone who wasn't always gone and had some stability in his life.

She ignored me, and before I knew anything about it, her and Lenny got married. They didn't have no big wedding or jump the broom or nothing like that, just went to the Justice of the Peace and got married. Lenny didn't even stay home on their wedding night. He told Andrea he had a train run to New York and would be back in the morning.

That next day after he got back from New York, Lenny moved into the house with us. He had been staying in a rooming house and didn't want Andrea to live in no dump. He didn't have to tell me because I wasn't about to let her live like that. He was the one who wanted to get away from that dump and Andrea was his ticket out. He had barely moved in good when he was gone somewhere again. She seemed to be under some kind of spell when it came to Lenny because something was very wrong. A husband she had just married hours before jumped on a train heading out of town and stayed gone for a week.

Andrea never knew when he was leaving or when he would be coming home. Yet she walked around going to work every day and coming home every night as if everything was all right. I knew no good could come out of their marriage because even thought the man stayed gone more than he was home, it seemed to me that he never had any money to show for it. More than once I heard him ask Andrea for money and she always gave it to him but I never once saw it go the other way around.

"If your husband is working all the time," I told her one day, "he should have lots of money and not need yours."

"Well I guess it might seem that way to you Cousin

Isaiah but Lenny can't help it because he has to buy food on the railroad and pay to keep his uniforms clean. Plus he owes money to some folks that he's paying off so we can save up and get our own house."

I knew better but I also knew Andrea wasn't going to listen to me so I didn't say anything else. She was in love, or at least believed she was, and in her case that was a bad thing.

Six months passed and I began to notice bruises on Andrea's arms. I asked her about them and she said one of the sick people she worked with had accidentally grabbed her too tight when she gave him a shot. As time went on, I noticed even more marks and bruises on her arms and neck and even one on her left cheek. I asked her flat out if Lenny had been hitting on her. She couldn't look me in my face when she answered, "No." That was how I knew she wasn't telling the truth. I had known her all her life and some things about her I knew better than she did herself.

The next day when I got off work, I sat down at the dining table with a cup of tea while Brook ate his dinner. He finished and sat there looking at me so I told him to say whatever was on his mind.

"Sometimes when you're not around, Lenny yells a lot at Andrea. About money and stuff. I think he be drunk. I stayed out of it 'cause I thought that must be what married people do, and then I…"

"And then you what?"

"And then I remembered you and your Bonnie. I know I was little back then, but I never heard the two of you carry on anything like that."

Hearing her name, the only thing I could say was, "Un hunh."

"Well, I mostly just ignored them until he started hitting on her."

"You saw him hit her?"

"No, they keep the room door closed and locked. You know he put a lock on it after they got married?"

"Yeah I know."

"So I didn't see it, but I know what it sound like when somebody get slapped or hit. When I knock on the door and ask them what's wrong, that's when it stops."

"How come you never say nothing before?"

"Andrea made me promise not to."

"Then how come you telling me now?"

"Because that was the wrong promise to make."

"Ok. Thank you."

With all the hell those children had been through, here was this slick Lenny putting them through even more. The first chance I got, I asked Andrea again about her bruises. When she lied again, I told her what Brook had said.

"He ain't had no right telling you my personal business. How dare he—"

"Girl is you done gone crazy? Your brother trying to look out for you and he told me because he scared for you."

"Y'all just don't want to see me happy 'cause you not happy! I don't have to live like that!"

"What kind'a fool talk is that?!"

"Just stay out'a my business and let me be happy for once in my life!"

She went to her room and slammed the door. I waited all week for Lenny to turn up and tried to talk with him too. I told him that if I ever heard tell that he hit Andrea again, he would have to kill me because I was sure going to kill him. Or at the very least I would hurt him so bad he'd never get over it. He had the nerve to look me dead in my eyes and smile when he spoke.

"Mr. Isaiah, I really don't think my precious Andrea would appreciate you threatening her husband. Can't you tell how much that girl love herself some Lenny?"

The only time I had ever been as mad as I was at that moment was when I found that rattlesnake in my baby's bed and cut its head off. That was exactly what I wanted to do to Lenny at that moment.

"Yeah, you right, she sure do love herself some Lenny. But she won't be the first broken-hearted widow to bury a no count nigger like you."

Lenny moved out of the house that same day. A week later Andrea moved out to be with him. I asked why she hadn't moved out the same day Lenny did. She said he'd been working all that time and had just gotten back but was getting ready to leave again. Why that made sense to her I couldn't say.

The two of them moved to a run down, rat-filled boarding house in one of the worst parts of D.C. That's where they were living when I found out that Andrea was about to have a baby. I went to the hospital where she worked and suggested she come back home.

"If my husband's not welcome in your house then I don't want to be there," she said.

"Your husband welcome long as he act like a man, not beatin' on you and takin' the money you earn but treatin' you the way a husband supposed to."

Andrea looked tired, like she hadn't been eating or taking care of herself. I noticed she had some new bruises on her body.

"Andrea, when someone loves you, they don't treat you like that. You old enough to remember your father and you never saw him hit your mother. You never saw me hit Bonnie. I'm begging you, stay away from Lenny and come back home. That place you're living in not someplace you ought'a be having a baby. You need to be in a clean house with people who love you and can help you."

"Thank you for your offer cousin Isaiah but no thank you. Now you'll have to excuse me while I get back to work. My patients are waiting for me."

I went back home without her. I thought maybe if I apologized to Lenny for talking so hard to him I might be able to put sense into his head, but that fool said he didn't need me or anything I had. This came from a man who didn't have a damn thing to his name and who had to beat a young woman to put a dollar in his pocket. I left them both alone and hoped in time they would come around. Again, I felt helpless knowing that there was nothing I could do.

Four months later, one of the nurses who worked with Andrea came to the house. As soon as I opened the door and saw her standing there, I knew something bad had happened. I just didn't know how bad it was. Why hadn't Andrea listened to me and come back home? Now this young lady was about to tell me something I knew was going to happen all along.

"I'm sorry to tell you this Mr. Jones but Andrea didn't show up for work a couple of days and that wasn't like her, so a couple of the nurses went this morning to her room at the boarding house and…and they found her dead sir. I'm sorry. I've seen you at the hospital talking with her, so I thought you should know as soon as possible."

"Anybody say how she died?"

"People at the boarding house said they heard her

and Lenny arguing and fighting. They said they did it so much that nobody thought it was anything unusual or worse than normal. Said they didn't realize Andrea had been beaten to death and thought she'd gone on to work like she always did. Now Lenny's gone and nowhere to be found."

"And…what about her baby miss? What about Andrea's baby?"

"Well, I'm afraid she never gave birth to it Mr. Jones. I'm so sorry."

"Thank you for telling me."

"Yes sir. Goodbye."

Lenny had killed his wife and child at the same time. How was it, I wondered, that God let people like him breathe the same air as me. Then I remembered that demon named Isaac who lived with us on the plantation. He was the first demon I'd ever met in the flesh, and yet Lew was his half-brother and had been like one of our angels.

Police said Lenny had gotten fired from his job with the railroad two months before, and they had no idea where he was. I looked for him myself but I never saw him again. If I ever do see him, I know I'll do something I'll regret later on. He'd even had the nerve to take every cent Andrea had in the bank out.

I buried her next to her mother and brother Will. It was mid May. Andrea's baby would have been born in July. An awful ache filled my eyes that day but again my tears refused to fall. All of this reminded me of Bonnie and Jamie and I found myself wondering why we had left the plantation again. Washington D.C. was killing us or making us kill ourselves. One at a time, we were all being eaten alive by this place. I told myself I had to be strong for Brook. No matter what, I had to go on.

# ♦ CHAPTER 19 ♦

Brook was all I had left of my family in this world. He was fifteen years old now. He had lost his mother, a brother, and his sister in D.C. It was a wonder that boy hadn't gone plum-mad himself. I was a full-grown man and at times thought I would go crazy myself if I wasn't already and just didn't know it. I guess having been a slave working in the fields on Woodloe Plantation from sun up to sun down made me stronger than I realized.
I don't know what it was but I kept doing what I had to do.

I went to my job every day and smiled at people who would throw paper on the floors just to see me pick it up. We weren't slaves anymore, but some white folks still wanted us to act like slaves. I would clean the "Whites Only" bathrooms and drinking fountains knowing that my black skin made it illegal for me to use them. Negroes were declared second-class citizens and told to be happy that we weren't slaves anymore.

As I went along with my work from day to day, I never complained, not even once. Where I had come from and what I had been through had been a whole lot worse.

So I did my work and went home at the end of the day to the only family I had left, my little cousin Brook. I spent a lot of time at home talking with him. Unlike his brother Will, Brook wanted nothing to do with life in the streets. He had seen what it did to his family just like I had and he wanted no part of it.

I asked Brook one day if he thought that we should go back to Savannah. He stood still for a long time and looked at me without saying a word. After a while, he asked, "Why would we want to do that? I'm never going back to the South. Why would I want to go back to the place where I was born a slave."

"Even though you were born a slave Brook you never had to work as one."

"I know I didn't go through the kinds of things you did Isaiah, but I've learned a lot about the difference between what it means to be a slave and what it means to be free. I know I was only six or seven years old when we left Savannah but I remember the rags we wore and called clothes. I remember the pallets we slept on and called beds, the shacks we called houses. But you know what I remember most of all?"

"Well I hope it's something good."

"No it ain't. I remember riding in the wagon on our way up here when you and mama tried to cover my eyes so I couldn't see those burned up dead bodies hanging from the trees. But we passed so many that she couldn't cover my eyes in time. And even when she did cover them, she couldn't stop the other people in their wagons from screaming at the sight of them. And she couldn't stop or hide that smell of burned human beings. I smell those bodies every day Isaiah. I can smell them right now. And besides that, you remember what mama used to say?"

"What's that?"

"She said no matter where we go in this world, sooner or later God gon take us out of it."

That was the most I'd ever heard Brook say in his life and I never asked him about going back to the South again.

It's a terrible thing to lose your family and start having doubts about the choices you made. All of this was hard on me so I knew it was twice as hard on Brook. From time to time I could see the sadness in his eyes. However, it didn't stop him from going on with his life. We had each other and I guess that was a good thing.

There were lots of days when I just wanted to give up. If it hadn't been for Brook, I might have just said to hell with it and gave up on trying to do anything at all. But Brook never gave up so I didn't either. He would tell me liquor wasn't going to get him, the streets weren't going to get him, and love wasn't going to get him. He was going to make something out of his life. There were many nights when I heard him in his room, crying long into the night until he fell asleep. I never let on that I heard him. I let him grieve in peace just like I used to grieve in peace.

I often wondered why so many bad things had happened to us. Why did all the people in my life have to die? Why were they all taken away from me and would Brook be next? If anyone had to go I hoped it would be me. I was close to thirty years old now and Brook would soon be turning seventeen. We were the only two people left in our family that we knew about. When we died, who would be left to tell people we had been slaves on Woodloe Plantation? Who would tell them how we had been freed, made our way to Washington D.C., and bought a home all our own? Then I thought back to those people that Brook had remembered hanging from the trees. The ones that the soldiers cut down and buried had unmarked graves and no one would remember them. Sure, someone might wonder about them from time to time but what good would that do?

All that thinking made my head hurt so I let it be.

### ♦ CHAPTER 20 ♦

Brook grew up to be a strong good-looking young man. He looked a lot like Fran and my mother so people would ask me if he was my son. I would tell them no and that he was my cousin. Each time this happened his eyes would get sad.

He really loved D.C. and became interested in politics and government and such. Some days he would come to the capital where I worked and spend all day listening to folks talk about laws and government and the country. To me it was just a lot of men wasting time sitting around all day doing nothing. Brook saw it differently and couldn't get enough of it. You would have thought heaven had opened and the boy was standing in front of the pearly gates.

He was learning about government at the college he went to and got involved with a group of students who ran a Negro newspaper. Folks called it the *Penny Paper* because it came out once a week and only cost a penny. The students who wrote it called it *The Negro's Voice*.

They wrote about everything from black people going back to Africa, to picking yourself up by your boot-straps to get ahead in life. They wrote about people like Frederick Douglass, who had been one of the most outspoken abolitionists anybody knew about.

The group was mainly students Brook's age and a little older that went to college with him. From time to time they would have meetings at each others' homes. I remember the first time they came to our house. After they had all been there for a while, Brook asked me to come in and introduce myself. I noticed there were a lot of pretty girls in the group and laughed to myself as I thought maybe that's why Brook had joined it. I guess if I'd been his age I might have joined that group too. But then come to think of it, I had already been a married man at that age and by the time I was a little older, I was a widower and a father who had buried his only child. That might have been why people asked if I was Brook's father instead of his brother or uncle or anything else. I was still fairly young in my early thirties but so much had happened in my life that I often spoke like somebody a lot older.

He introduced me as cousin Isaiah. After that everyone called me, "Cousin Isaiah." Some of them had come from slaves like us but some of them had not. Their families had been free before the war. They asked me questions about my life on Woodloe and the trip from Savannah to D.C. I hadn't expected that and so gave a few answers and then excused myself.

Once everybody had gone home I asked Brook which one of the girls he fancied. He said none of them, but I knew better. I remembered being in love and I remembered that dumb look you got on your face when someone asked you about it. I saw that same look on

Brook's face. I let it be and didn't ask him anymore about it.

He said he wanted to become a writer and write for the Washington newspaper. I told him I didn't know if they had any Negro writers, but if he put his mind to it I knew he could be the first. I also told him how I went to work everyday from Monday thru Friday and how the white folks who worked in the offices never spoke to me except for when and if I said, "Good morning." They would hardly look at me as they answered back and some wouldn't even bother to answer. None of them ever called me by my name or asked me what it is. It was always, "janitor this, or clean-up man that." I think the only white person that knew my name was my supervisor, but I wouldn't bet on it.

Some of the Negroes I worked with and ate lunch with knew it. I really never got too close to any of them either. They all drank and such and I had no interest in any of that. So for years I went to work unnoticed, unheard, and unseen, going about doing my work, keeping my mouth shut, and coming home. Brook said if I could do it for all those years he was sure he could do it working at the Washington paper. In the meantime, he wrote for the *Penny Paper*.

Once he wrote about how we as Negroes were grouped into different social and money classes. It seemed like because we owned a house and I had a job mopping floors and cleaning toilets for the government we were what people called middle class. Rich folks were upper class and poor folks they called lower class. I had seen this on the plantations in the South too but had never thought about it the way Brook wrote about it. In my mind, it was house slaves and field slaves all over again.

I had noticed how some lighter complexioned Negroes acted like they didn't want to be around the darker Negroes. Some white folks would treat the lighter skinned Negroes different also. It was a bunch of silliness to me, one person thinking he was better than the next just because he was able to eat a little more or dress a little fancier. It didn't make no kind of sense to me. Where us black folks were concerned, we all had come out of slavery. Well most of us anyway. I guess old juke-joint Joe back in Savannah had been upper class since he dressed and ate better than a lot of people. But that didn't get him anything but dead, which was why I didn't see any need to be put in no class.

Then Brook said it wasn't just Negroes who were put into classes. Whites were too. He didn't really know anything about the white folks who had worked on the plantation with us because he'd been too young for the fields himself. He hadn't seen how poor they were, but I had so I already knew there were rich ones and poor ones. I also saw them every day walking around D.C. Even though some of them were dirt poor, they still acted like they were above Negroes. I mean they could be dirt poor and hungry and still call you "nigger" to make their selves feel bigger. The ones that came up North with us did that. I felt sorry for them and I wanted many times to give them food. I didn't though. I just left them to themselves the same as I did most of the black folks traveling along. I knew if they knew we had something they would try to take it. If that's what being in different classes was all about, then it was just a fact of life to me.

Brook on the other hand wanted to change all that. It was how things had always been, I told him, and it was probably the way they would always be. Things took time to change. If it took years for them to become the way they were, it would take years for them to become something different.

To hear Brook talk about making folks change their way of thinking made me worry. Not a day went by that I didn't think about the effect of our family's tragedies on him, and now I had even more reason to be concerned. White folks didn't like change and they really didn't like no Negroes talking about being the ones to make the changes. They liked things just the way they had them. The last time I'd heard any big talk about change was just before the Civil War got started. I just knew that little *Penny Paper* he was writing for would make some folks mad sooner or later. I just hoped they wouldn't get so mad they'd come after Brook. How many folks read the paper I didn't know, but figured not too many white folks paid it any attention. I sure hoped they didn't.

As time went on I became a little more relaxed about the situation. I stayed relaxed until the day I heard about the protests. Now I had never heard of a protest before, and it didn't seem like a good thing to me. The students were angry and talking out in public about how things weren't right. It was something about white folks counting Negroes as three-fifths of a man.

"It don't matter what people count you as so long as you know what you are and so long as it's not 'no-count,'" I told Brook.

"It matters when it comes to voting and being represented by the government cousin Isaiah. A whole man should be counted as a whole man and it shouldn't take two men to be counted as one and then have some left over from a third man."

"Have some left over? How's that possible?"

"It's not, and that's the point, the whole thing doesn't make any sense."

Sometimes Brook got real upset with me and said I was still thinking like a slave instead of like a free man who was a citizen of the United States of America. He used the words "citizens" and "equality" a lot when he wrote for the newspaper and when he talked with me. He'd get about as fired up as some of those preachers down in Savannah except they'd been talking about religion and he was all excited over his favorite words "democracy" and "citizenship" and "equality."

I just knew it was going to turn into big trouble. I could feel it deep down in my soul. Too much education without enough common sense understanding to go along with it can be a bad thing. Sometimes the things you know can hurt you or get you hurt.

I never was too clear on exactly what happened to Brook. My understanding is that a group of students went to downtown D.C. and started going up and down the street offering them *Penny Papers* for free to everybody passing by. Then some of them started reading it and didn't like what they read. Seems like they either got scared or mad, or the got real interested and started standing around talking about the paper.

One group of Whites didn't like what they read or said at all. They started shouting until someone threw a rock. Then came another rock and a store window got broken to pieces. Next thing you know, you had Whites and Blacks going at it right in downtown D.C. in broad daylight. Some of the white folks were fighting on the same side as the black ones and some of the black folks against each other. Soldiers came to break it all up. Out of all this, three people were killed. All of them were Negroes. One of them was Brook. I told that boy that he couldn't change things if people didn't want the change.

Now those Negroes telling me he's a martyr. What the hell is that, some fancy word for fool? I had lost everybody I had in my family and those folks couldn't even tell me who had killed Brook. I don't know if it was the angry Whites who killed him, the soldiers, or one of his own people. All I knew was that he was dead and he had been right about one thing. The streets didn't kill him, and liquor didn't kill him, nor did love. He never learned that sometimes change takes time, a lot of time. People hadn't just learned how to hate over night. It took them years to learn how to hate and it would take them years to learn how not to hate. None of that mattered now because Brook was dead.

# ♦ CHAPTER 21 ♦

On a cold day in February, I buried Brook with his mother Fran, his sister Andrea, and his brother Will. My hands and feet stayed cold that entire day. All of Brook's friends and a lot of people I didn't know came to his funeral. Some of them even spoke about him. They had written about him in their newspaper and said he wouldn't be forgotten. They made him out to be some kind of hero or something. None of that changed the way I felt. I just didn't know what to do with my feelings. So after the funeral I took a long walk around the city.

As I walked, my mind raced and I couldn't control my thoughts. I remembered the places we all would visit together and all the things we had done over the years. I asked myself again if I should leave Washington. At least in Savannah there were some people still there that I knew growing up. Here I was by myself with no one left but me. For the first time in my life, I was truly alone and scared of becoming a lonely old man with nobody. It seemed like most of my life someone had depended on me. Now they were all gone, I had no one. I began to think that a soul could only be free in death. Walking around Washington for the better part of that night, I remembered the times I had gone looking for Will and Fran, and that damn no-count Lenny. There are no words to describe the pain I felt inside. My heart was filled with sorrow, I could feel the hurt down in my bones, but it wasn't sorrow for me. It was for the family I had been unable to save. No matter what I had done or how I had done it, they all ended up dead. I hoped that my ancestors would forgive me for failing them all. I looked up at the night sky and I asked them if they would.

Just before daylight I went on home and got into bed. I decided not to go to work that day. Later on, I got up again and went in the kitchen to make some breakfast. For some reason, I wanted sweetbread and buttermilk that morning. As I sat at the table listening to the silence of the house and thinking about how lonely the house was, someone knocked on the door. Could that be death coming to take me away too? I felt numb as I walked slowly toward the door.

When I opened the door, there was the group of kids that wrote the *Penny Paper* with Brook. I asked them what they wanted and they said they had come to check on me. The only people who'd ever checked on me before were Aunt Fran and Bonnie, so I didn't know what to say. Them kids walked right in my house and started cleaning and fixing up things like I had invited them in to do it.

That was forty odd years ago, and I still haven't got rid of them. I watched them mature and have children of their own. And then I watched their children grow up and start having families. It seemed like they had all made some kind promise with Brook that they would look after me if anything happened to him. Whenever I came home from work, some of them would be around. They were always inviting me to go here or there. Sometimes I would go and sometimes I would just stay home. They would fix food for me, or would ask me to tell them stories about life on the plantation. Sometimes they would tell me about what they were doing at the time.

One of them, named Josiah Wilson, started a newspaper of his own called *The Negro American Weekly*. Naturally I was skeptical about that. Then he brought me a copy of it one week not too long after it started and what did I see right there on the front page but a picture somebody had drawn of me. It was sitting big as everything right next to an article called "Isaiah Jones and His Family."

"What the…"

I looked at Josiah. He was a big strapping fellow who looked more like a lumberjack or something instead of a newspaper man. He smiled and shrugged his shoulders. Then I started reading.

The story was all about how I had grown up in slavery until freedom came when I was fifteen, and how I had lost part of my family down South, then made my way to D.C. and lost the rest of my family. They said that through it all I had remained an example of a strong black man who'd made many sacrifices in the struggle to take care of my family. According to the story, everybody who knew me considered me to be a living symbol of grace and faith. I thought that sounded more like Bonnie than me. It ended with them saying how the black men of my generation had brought them this far since freedom came and how it was up to them to take the race and the country even further so the pain and sacrifices of men like me would not be in vain.

That story took up most of the front page and then half of another page on the inside. What in the world was I supposed to think about that?

Needless to say I never did leave D.C. I guess it was because of Brook and his friends. The truth of the matter is I don't know what I would do without them. However, I'll never tell them that. Besides it turned out they needed me as much as I needed them. Who else was going to tell them how to change people, and get what you want, a little at a time? After all, we had become free, and that was one of the biggest changes of all.

Some days they tried to pair me up with this or that lady. But Bonnie was the only woman I had known and the only one I cared to know. They'd have them ladies come cook for me or bring sweets by the house. They were nice so I sat and talked with them. Sometimes I enjoyed the time I spent with them. Only I had become too afraid to love anybody or anything the way I had Bonnie. Couldn't stand the thought of them being taken away too. Besides, the kids don't know that a lot of nights I don't sleep. I sit in my house and think about the people that I lost. Sometimes I hear their voices around the house. I sure do miss them, and I hope they knew I loved them, and that I still do.

It's like Miss Lizzy said, "still waters do run deep." All my life I have been like still waters. You can't just look and tell how deep they run. People only saw me from the outside. I wanted to shed a lot of tears over the years that I lived, but no one ever saw me do that. I just had to be there for everyone else. After all I was the head of the family, they all depended on me. So I held back my tears and I never gave up.

It took a while but I finally figured out what Miss Lizzy did that day I went to get the medicine for Bonnie, when she put a bottle under my eyes and caught the tears that I couldn't cry any more. The tears I wanted to shed but that wouldn't fall. She knew that I had to be the strong one, the one to hold the family together. If she's still alive I hope Miss Lizzy still has those tears. I hope she has them in one of her little bottles marked Isaiah's tears. I hope she still remembers me.

If you read my words I don't want you to feel sorry for any of us. Because unlike so many people before us, we all found out what being free was. We were free to live our lives the way we saw fit. We were free to learn the things that we learned and to make the mistakes that we made. We were free to go where we chose to go and to live where we chose to live. Life might not have always been good all the time but it wasn't always bad either. Compared to many I think that we had good lives because despite all the heartbreaks we got to live them according to our own choices and desires, and I'm thankful for that. I'm thankful for every year that I lived and every soul that I helped along the way.

Now you know why I wrote these words on paper. So that when I die someone might read this and remember us. Isaiah, Fran, Andrea, Will, Brook, Bonnie, Jamie, and the many others like us who were born as slaves and became free. Never to be slaves again.